"Of course I'm not going to stop you from leaving, June. But I have to tell you, I don't think it's safe, and I'd really rather you not put yourself in any more danger than you already have today."

Ignoring the fact that this man shouldn't care about her well-being so much, June ran through all of her options in her head—all zero of them. She sighed. He was right. She was stuck there for the foreseeable future. She'd never in her life experienced such a dangerous storm, and she definitely didn't know how to safely travel in one. Besides, she had the puppies to think of now. The minute she'd picked them up, they'd become her responsibility, and she couldn't just abandon them with a doctor who had other patients to care for, especially one who was only temporarily managing his father's clinic.

She looked up at Dr. Singh, who appeared almost as uneasy as she.

"I hate to break it to you, June, but under the circumstances, the smartest thing for you to do is to spend the night here with me."

* * *

PEACH LEAF, TEXAS: Where true love blooms

Dear Reader,

I live in Texas, and it's no secret that we have some of the warmest weather in the country. So, when we get snow here in the South, it's often a welcome escape from the heat...unless things get crazy! Which is exactly what happens in this, the latest in my Peach Leaf, Texas series.

When an uncanny blizzard blows into town and June Leavy finds a couple of puppies alone in the cold, she and sweet, handsome veterinarian Ethan Singh must work together to take care of their adorable charges. Along the way, Ethan and June find themselves falling in love with more than just the tiny balls of fur in their care.

I absolutely adore stories in which a hero and heroine are forced together by circumstances outside their control, and then, as the clock ticks by, they realize they aren't ready to part ways when their problems are solved. I hope you have a wonderful time watching Ethan and June work together to save the lives of two fuzzy friends, and of course, fall in love.

And the next time you find yourself snuggled up in a snowstorm, I wish you warmth, companionship and, most important, love.

Very best,

Amy Woods

Puppy Love
for the Veterinarian

—

Amy Woods

Recycling programs
for this product may
not exist in your area.

ISBN-13: 978-0-373-65970-8

Puppy Love for the Veterinarian

Copyright © 2016 by Amy Woods

This edition published by arrangement with Harlequin Books S.A.

For questions and comments about the quality of this book, please contact us at CustomerService@Harlequin.com.

Printed in U.S.A.

Amy Woods took the scenic route to becoming an author. She's been a bookkeeper, a high school English teacher and a claims specialist, but now that she makes up stories for a living, she's never giving it up. She grew up in Austin, Texas, and lives there with her wonderfully goofy, supportive husband and a spoiled rescue dog. Amy can be reached on Facebook, Twitter and her website, amywoodsbooks.com.

Books by Amy Woods

Harlequin Special Edition

Peach Leaf, Texas

An Officer and Her Gentleman
His Pregnant Texas Sweetheart
Finding His Lone Star Love
His Texas Forever Family

Visit the Author Profile page
at Harlequin.com for more titles.

This one is for the animal rescuers;
thank you for the wonderful lives you save.
And for my Maggie dog, who has my heart.

Chapter One

"June, hon, why don't you go on home now? I can finish closing up here myself, and it looks like things may get worse than they originally predicted."

June Leavy looked up from her mop bucket and followed the owner of Peach Leaf Pizza's eyes to the small television behind the counter, tuned in to the evening weather segment. January in west Texas could be unpredictable, but the idea of the twelve to eighteen inches of snow the meteorologist called for actually covering the ground and sticking was just surreal.

She studied her boss's face, not missing the lines around Margaret's mouth and the shadowy thumb-prints beneath the older woman's usually lively eyes. It had been a busy day, amid a busy week; they were both exhausted, but the work would be completed much faster with two pairs of hands.

June shook her head, causing a few more strands of hair to escape her ponytail. "Nonsense. I'm almost finished with the floor, and then all that's left is taking out the garbage."

Margaret offered a weary smile as her thanks, but June could see the relief in her boss's face. She would never admit it, but Margaret Daw was getting older. It was time for her to retire and June could feel that the day was coming when her boss would ask her to take over. Margaret had all but asked her about it on more than one occasion—who could blame a new grandma for wanting to spend more time with the adorable twin babies recently born to her pediatrician son and daughter-in-law?—and besides, June was her only full-time employee and comanager. In many ways, it just made sense.

June sighed and sloshed the mop back into the gray water, wondering again how she would respond if and when the day arrived. She could see the pros and cons list she'd pored over so many times in her mind's eye, her options jotted out clear as day on the yellow pad sitting next to the remote control on her coffee table. But no matter how many times she mulled over the bullet points, the decision wouldn't be easy.

Margaret was a wonderful boss—kind and fair— and the job provided steady income. There was something comforting in the daily tasks, in kneading the dough each morning, chopping fresh vegetables and taking orders, in the warm, familiar faces of Peach Leaf Pizza's many regular customers. She would miss the banter, catching up with people she'd known her whole life and the excitement in kids' faces when they piled into the red leather booths after winning baseball games or performing well in dance recitals.

But she had dreams of her own, too.

And until recently, June had been so close to turning them into reality. So close, in fact, that the bruises from losing everything hadn't yet healed.

Now her choice was between picking up the pieces and starting over—letting herself believe that she could somehow regain what was lost—or sticking with the safe option, taking over the pizza parlor and borrowing her neighbors' joy as they lived their lives.

Put that way, it didn't seem like much of a choice at all, but she reminded herself that starting over wouldn't exactly guarantee a happy ending, either.

"Back to square one," she said aloud without meaning to.

"What's that?" Margaret called from the counter.

"Oh... I was just wondering if it's really going to get as bad as they're saying."

She tilted her chin at the television, where the Austin meteorologist gesticulated animatedly, her arms waving in circles and lines to indicate high and low pressure points across a multicolored map of Texas.

"Beats me." Margaret shrugged, her shoulders tapping the pizza-slice painted earrings she wore so that they swirled around beneath her silvery curls. "Wouldn't be the first time, though, you know."

June finished cleaning a blotch of spilled marinara and pushed the wheeled bucket toward the back of the shop, doing a once-over of the black-and-white checked tiles in case she missed a spot.

Margaret wiped the last bit of counter and stood on her tiptoes to turn off the TV before removing her apron. "When I was a girl, we got a couple of feet out at our house, and I'll tell you, it is no easy time getting around town in that much powder." She put a hand on one hip and pointed at June with the other. "Especially when nobody around here knows how to drive in that stuff."

Nodding her agreement, June crossed the kitchen and emptied the mop bucket into the designated sink, then shoved the cleaning supplies into a broom closet. She supposed it was possible that the weather might take a turn for the worse—it had been snowing steadily for a few days, so there was already a little covering the ground—but the thought of that much more coming down in the span of just a few hours in their neck of Texas still somehow didn't seem re-alistic. Sure, they got a few inches most years, and there was always the danger of ice, especially on the country roads outside of town, but she didn't think there was too much to worry about. She was certain she had plenty of time to get home before anything major hit.

But when she closed the supply closet door and turned around, June found Margaret looking up at her from all of nearly five feet, her boss's clear blue eyes fully of worry beneath a forehead creased with concern.

"Just promise me you'll be extra careful, and if it gets bad, we won't open tomorrow. Just stay home. I don't want you getting hurt trying to make it into work, you hear?"

June gave a reassuring smile, promised that she'd be safe and patted Margaret's shoulder. Over the years, their relationship had deepened into more than just a typical owner/employee situation. Her boss treated her more like a daughter than a paid worker, which only made things harder when thinking about the next chapter of her life. She knew Margaret would hate the idea of June factoring her needs into future plans, but they *were* a factor. A big one. If she ever got back on her feet, if she ever found a way to get back all the money she'd spent years carefully saving to open her own bakery, she would have to leave someone she cared about, someone who'd helped see her through the lowest point of her life. That mattered. Deeply.

She shook her head. There was no use thinking about it now.

The money was gone. In all likelihood, that meant her dreams were gone with it. She'd worked herself to the bone for over a decade earning it and had gone without quite a few comforts to save until it amounted to enough to buy her own bakeshop. Her shoulders sunk as the weight of loss settled once again. It would take years before she could build her former financial stability and credit back up, and even more to get her savings back.

Six months had passed since Clayton left, taking everything with him. Their money. Hers, really, if she were being honest, and she was now—too much had happened for anything less. Her dreams.

And, last but not least, her heart.

Even after all he'd done, taking the cash from their joint account and running off to gamble it away in Vegas, June thought there might be a place inside of her that still missed that stupid man. It wasn't that she loved him still—no, he'd broken her trust and hurt her far too much for that to be the case—but the loss of him and all they'd shared, and the deep chasm of loneliness in his wake, the death of the life they'd built together... June thought maybe those were the things she truly mourned. And it wasn't that she needed him, either, or any man, for that matter. She'd been single for most of her life until Clayton came along and had been happy and fulfilled before his presence.

But that was just it. Until he left, she would have sworn to anyone that he was the one she'd spend the rest of her life with, and when he'd gone, all those promises of a family and a life with him vanished, and she was back where she'd been before—only this time, it wasn't the same. This time, she knew what it was like to share her home with someone she loved, to talk about having kids one day and to dream together, staring off into the future, side by side. This time, she felt the absence.

Shoulders up, chin up, she told herself, remembering Margaret's wise words in the aftermath of that mess. Better to make peace with the present, than to dwell on the past, right?

Of course.

Starting with her small, albeit cozy, apartment, June forced herself to make a list of all of the things she had to be grateful for. When she finished, she headed back to the storefront and kitchen to fetch the two large trash bags, hefting them over her shoulders to carry through the restaurant to the Dumpster in the loading area out back.

Things weren't so very bad. She had her job, her friends and a warm place to live, and for that she was thankful. It was a good thing right now to be single and free, to have time and space to decide what to do next, what path to take in putting her life back together. No strings, no one else to care for, no one to put before her own needs. She planned on staying that way for a good while; it would take someone very special to convince her to put her trust in a relationship again, and she was fairly convinced that person might not be anywhere in her future, near or far. It was a…difficult thought to swallow, but one she was doing her best to accept.

June dropped the trash bags near the back door and went to get her coat. Margaret was doing the same. "Bundle up, now."

"Yes, ma'am," she teased, holding her fingers to her forehead in a salute.

Margaret put both hands on her hips, a foreboding

figure. "I'm not joking around, Junie. You forget I'm from upstate New York, where it gets dangerously cold in the winter. You Texans don't know from cold, and you're always caught unawares when it hits. Don't let it get the best of you."

"Okay, I promise."

Both women pulled on gloves, hats and purses, and Margaret opened the back door for June when she picked up the garbage bags. A blast of frigid air slapped her across the face and briefly challenged her footing until she steadied herself against its force.

"I'm good here, Marg. I'll drop these off and lock up. See you in the morning," she shouted over her shoulder as she stepped onto the loading dock and into what felt like gale-force winds.

"I'm not so sure about that."

June chuckled to herself. "Okay, then, see you soon."

"All right, hon. Don't forget what I said about not coming in if it's bad," Margaret called, her voice fading as the back door slammed behind her and she headed for her car in the front parking lot, which she always parked next to June's fifteen-year-old jalopy.

June shook her head at the older woman's cosseting, then heaved the bags into the giant metal bin, starting at the loud clanging sound that erupted.

Something else must have heard it, too, and re-acted the same way, because June caught motion in her peripheral vision as she turned back to lock up the door. Her heart jumped into her throat, and it fluttered there like so many trapped butterflies as she spun quickly to take in her surroundings.

"Hello?"

She listened carefully and heard…nothing, except maybe her own pulse pounding at her temples.

"Is anyone out here?" she called again, reaching into her purse for her pocketknife and cell phone. There was probably nothing to worry about. This was Peach Leaf, after all, where the running crime rate was pretty much zilch. All the same, she was a woman alone in an alley after dark, so it was only smart to be cautious.

Scanning the view once more to make certain she wasn't about to be attacked, June decided that instead of locking the back door and walking around front to her little car as she usually did, she'd just go through the store.

That was when she heard something again. A quiet rustling, followed by what sounded like a series of soft squeaks. She closed her eyes for just a few seconds, trying to decide whether or not to ignore the sound, knowing the wise thing to do was to walk away. Whatever it was, it was not her problem, and Lord knew she did not need any of those in her life just then.

But then she heard it again, and this time, the soft, sad little cries were like warm fingers squeezing her heart. As the snow began to fall harder, flakes catching in her eyelashes and forming a thin, shawl-like layer on the red fabric of her coat, June released a great sigh and made the decision to investigate.

Whatever was making that noise—*please don't let it be a baby of any kind*, she thought—did not belong out there in a lonely alley on a freezing winter's night.

With the garbage bags out of her hands, June now pulled her coat closer around her and closed all four toggles before carefully descending the loading dock steps. A thin layer of ice had already formed, and she had no intention of tumbling down and breaking a bone or two. She pulled her purse strap up from her shoulder and over her head to secure it tightly, then dug out her cell phone, turning on the flashlight app. Its slim, bright beam shot out into the dark, and June crept slowly behind the pizza shop's garbage bin, the light illuminating nothing but a coating of grimy snow. She stopped and waited a moment, listening for the sound again so she could follow it to its source. Just as she was about to restart her search, she heard it again; this time, it was more distinct.

Placing a palm behind her ear, June tried to zero in on what it was—a kitten, maybe? Something small and helpless and lost? Again, she pleaded that it wouldn't be a baby. The thought of someone leaving a little one behind their restaurant, especially in this weather, was just…unthinkable.

There it was again, and now she was certain it was some sort of cry. Rolling her eyes upward in a silent prayer, she braced herself and started off in the direction of the noise, continuing as it became louder and louder, which meant she must be close. She was halfway down the alley, almost to the street, when she reached it, hidden in a dark corner behind another garbage bin.

Shining her flashlight into the shadows, June gasped, cold air filling her lungs and what felt like the rest of her body. The hand that wasn't holding her phone flew to her mouth as she looked into two pairs of big, brown eyes.

Big, brown…puppy eyes.

The squeaking, she now realized, was the heart-wrenching sound of tiny little canine yips, probably calling for their mother.

There, cuddled together in a heap of trash behind another store's Dumpster, were two itty-bitty bodies coated in black fur, with eight little white, black-spotted boots. But their tiny faces were the clincher. June's eyes filled with moisture, not from the biting air, as she stared at two pairs of fuzzy black ears, each separated down the middle by a thin line of white fur that traced down into identical white muzzles.

For a full minute, June remained frozen in place, her instinct telling her to rush forward and gather the pups in her arms to warm them up, but she wasn't yet positive on what was the right thing to do.

On the one hand, the temperatures had probably dropped to below freezing when the sun had disappeared—at least, it sure felt that way—but on the other, well, what if the puppies' mother returned, looking for them? What if she was around there somewhere and returned to find them gone? But the more pressing question was, of course—what if she didn't? The little ones couldn't have been out there for too long; otherwise they'd be...

No, she didn't want to think about that. Yet... that would certainly be the outcome if she didn't get the little dogs out of the cold, and quick. She could always check the alley the next day and put up flyers to find out if anyone had seen a female dog wandering around the strip mall or a suspicious person dropping off a little bundle. But for now, if she didn't get them out of the increasingly cold night air—and the snow that seemed to be falling faster and thicker each minute—they would surely freeze to death. Not much of a choice there.

Having made up her mind, June hurried forward and opened her coat, then picked up the puppies very gently and with extreme care, and tucked them into the front pouch of her Peach Leaf Pizza sweatshirt. She wrapped her coat across her middle, leaving it unfastened so they could breathe, and, head down, turned the corner out of the alley.

The wind was much fiercer without the protection of the buildings, and the several yards to her car seemed more like miles as June trudged through the now-blinding wind and snow in the direction of the front parking lot. Finally, she reached her car and pulled her keys from her purse to unlock the doors. Opening the trunk, she retrieved her gym bag and slammed down the lid, sliding into the backseat as quickly as possible. She pulled the door shut—no easy feat against the wind—and took a deep breath before unzipping the bag. She took out her jogging clothes and shoes, leaving her towel to make a sort of nest. Opening her coat, she removed the little balls of fluff and placed them carefully inside, close against each other for warmth.

"There," she said. "You guys hang on tight. We're going for help."

Satisfied with the answering squeaks, June pulled a seat belt around the bag and fastened it, hoping it would do, and then crawled into the front seat. Thankfully, her old car started after just a couple of tries, and she was able to pull out of the parking lot.

Snow fell in sheets as she made her way onto the main road with her blinkers on full blast, sifting through her memory for any winter-weather driving advice Margaret might have offered over the years, sorry that she hadn't listened more closely.

Wrapping the fore- and middle fingers of her left hand together for luck as she gripped the wheel with white knuckles, June set off to the only place she could think of that might be able to help her with two very fresh puppies.

Chapter Two

Ethan Singh cursed before his father's absurdly messy monster of a desk. One of these days, he promised himself for the hundredth time, he would have to suck it up and organize the damn thing. One of these days.

But not today. Or tonight, he supposed, strolling from the office and past the empty receptionist's desk to glance out the front window of his father's veterinary clinic, only mildly surprised to find a dark sky staring back. It was almost a relief to know that, as soon as he arrived at his parents' home and ate a quick dinner, it would be past time to head straight to bed.

Straight to bed meant no time to think about what he was doing in Peach Leaf, Texas, for the winter, and more importantly, what he would do when the season was over and it was time to head back to campus in Colorado, where he was scheduled to teach several veterinary classes over the spring semester.

Ethan gave his head a little shake and turned back from the window. It wouldn't do to ruminate on that now. The whole point in coming here, agreeing to run Dad's clinic while his parents took a one-month, long-overdue vacation to visit his father's brother in Washington, DC, was to *not* think about what happened in Alaska. Ethan sat down in the receptionist's seat and put his head in his hands. How could he not think about it? How could he not think about *her*—about what she'd done to break his heart into a thousand tiny shreds?

It was impossible.

He had looked forward to that research trip with great enthusiasm, knowing he'd get to spend every day with Jessica Fields, the incredibly intelligent and physically stunning colleague he'd been dating for a couple of weeks, following her recent arrival at his department at the university. And he'd gotten everything he wanted. Their time in northernmost Alaska, a place he'd learned both to love and respect for its extreme beauty and danger, had been absolutely perfect. The team's research on the impact of climate change and infectious disease in polar bears advanced far beyond what they'd initially anticipated, and so had his relationship with Jessica.

It wasn't until their final day that she'd begun to show signs of unease that any scientist worth his salt would have noticed. When he'd leaned in to kiss her on the flight back to Colorado, an action that at that point in their time together had become common-place, Jessica had pulled away, and he confronted her.

She wasn't single, she said, her eyes full of regret but not, he'd noted sadly, remorse. She was engaged to marry her college sweetheart and had no plans to break it off on account of what she called a "fling." She had led him on, she said.

Well, on that point he certainly would not argue. Sleeping with him, telling him she loved him, mak-ing plans with him…yes, he'd say she was damn right that she'd led him on. Ethan had immediately requested an alternative seat on the airplane, endur-ing the remainder of the flight with a clenched jaw, knotted stomach and the blinding urge to scream at the woman who had, in the space of a few months, turned his life upside down, and then quickly and heartlessly destroyed him.

The department head, though confused at his hasty, fictional explanation, had granted Ethan's re-quest for a short sabbatical, a semester off. Ethan hadn't taken a vacation since accepting the position five years before, and he supposed he was due a break. Though it hurt, not to get started right away on compiling and writing up the Alaskan data for conference presentations. He would never forget the way his breath had caught and his heartbeat raced as he'd knelt next to one of those regal bears to take a blood sample before the tranquilizer wore off. They were the most beautiful creatures he'd ever seen; they deserved saving and he would spend the rest of his life working to do just that.

He pushed out a breath, lifting his head to stare out the window once more as he listened to wind that had begun to swirl and howl. For now, he needed time—even just a few months—to figure out how to go back to the university and face Jessica, who had made it clear she had no plans to leave the team, despite what she'd done to him. He needed to come to terms with the fact that the only woman he'd ever fallen for was getting married to someone else and, worst of all, didn't seem to give a single damn what it would do to him.

In the meantime, he had the clinic, and over the past two weeks, he had to admit, he'd become fond of the locals and their beloved pets, and even of his house calls to care for a few horses and cattle on nearby ranches. He'd always loved the research part of being a veterinary pathologist, but this...this change of pace and reminder of where his career had begun, was nice, too, at least for now.

Ethan's head jerked up at the sound of raucous banging. It took him a minute to realize that it was coming from the front door, which he'd locked an hour ago after closing. Who on earth could be knocking— no, pounding—on the door now? Ethan knew that his father occasionally extended his workday beyond its normal twelve hours when a special circumstance arose, but no one had called to say they'd be coming in late or anything of the like.

He got up from the chair quickly, leaving it swiveling as he paced to the door. Whoever stood on the front stoop wasn't visible from the window he'd been looking out before, and the blinds were pulled down on the other side to cover the spot where the sun hit in late afternoon; he'd have to get much closer and peer through them to identify his visitor.

Ethan rolled his eyes. Yes, it was his duty to help out the local animal population in any way he could, but the day had already been particularly trying— several regular exams on top of two challenging, back-to-back house calls—and he practically ached to warm up a frozen meal, shower away the fur and jump into the cozy bed in his parents' guest room.

When he got to the door, he slid a finger between two blinds and peered out, but the snow was quite thick now, surprisingly so, and the visitor so bundled up that he couldn't make out anything other than the bright crimson of a coat and matching hat. He didn't even see any animals. But the wind was so fierce, and the snow falling in such a thick blanket, that he was compelled to open the door and let the poor person in, reminding himself that this was Peach Leaf, therefore generally void of a large city's potential threats.

Bracing himself, Ethan unlocked and pulled open the door, breath rushing from his lungs as the icy air hit. A tall figure rushed forward, nearly pummeling him to get inside the building, and for a second he regretted his decision to be kind.

"Oh, thank you," came a voice, definitely a woman's,

from somewhere in the depths of the coat and beanie. Ethan closed the door behind her.

"Thank you so, so much for letting me in. I thought there might not be anyone here this late and I was about to turn around and go back to my car, but…"

"Whoa, there. Hang on just a minute. Let's start at the beginning. How does that sound?" He clasped his hands in front of his abdomen and gave her some space.

The woman stopped speaking and pulled up her hat, which had fallen down into her face, nearly covering what he now saw were large, green—a very lovely green, in fact—eyes. "I'm sorry," she said, pushing out a puff of air. She reached out a gloved hand in Ethan's direction and he took it, startled to discover how cold it was.

She must be absolutely frozen from head to toe. He'd checked the thermometer that afternoon and, even before the sun had gone down, the temperature was below freezing. If he hadn't let her in, she might have been in real trouble. His semester in Alaska had taught him plenty about the dangers of extreme cold, and even though they were in Texas, which was generally mild, the hazards were the same if one wasn't careful. It didn't matter that the weather was out of the norm; it simply was, and therefore caution would need to be observed.

He hadn't anticipated things getting so bad, and hadn't much of a chance to pay attention to the forecast other than his brief check on the internet as he'd scarfed down a sandwich earlier, but now he could see plainly that the winter storm the meteorologists predicted had escalated quickly.

The woman pumped his hand up and down a few times before letting it go. "I'm June. June Leavy. I came by on the slim chance that Dr. Singh might still be here this late, and, well, I didn't really know what else to do."

"I'm Dr. Singh," Ethan said, doing his best to offer a warm smile despite feeling anything but.

The woman—June—narrowed her eyes and tilted her head to study him, chuckling softly. "Wow, Dr. Singh, I have to say, you look like you've stumbled upon the elusive fountain of youth."

Ethan had to laugh at that. Most folks, unless their pets were ill or aging, only came in for annual check-ups and vaccinations. It made sense that the senior Dr. Singh would not have had a chance to inform all clients of his winter vacation plans.

"No, I mean, I am Dr. Singh, but perhaps not the one you'd hoped to find. I'm his son Ethan."

June's face visibly relaxed as realization hit and she nodded, then proceeded to remove her gloves and hat. As she grasped her lapels and moved to take off her coat, Ethan noticed the bit of roundness at her middle and the thought crossed his mind that she might be pregnant. "Here, let me help you with that," he said, taking her coat.

He couldn't help but catch the subtle, sweet scent of her hair as he pulled the red fabric from her shoulders. Like melon, he thought. Odd that he should even notice. Odder still he should notice that it tumbled down her shoulders in soft, auburn waves, framing a face, he could see after he'd turned back from hanging her coat on an iron rack near the door, that was rosy from the cold and, well, quite lovely.

June smiled, and it occurred to Ethan that she was aptly named. Her skin was as bright as sunshine and the curve of her wide mouth heated his insides, head to toe. Her eyes were lively and warm like summer, although…her smile didn't quite reach them.

Not that he cared, though. Pure observation—like you'd get from any good scientist.

"Thank you," she said. "Now, as I was saying, I drove here on my way home from work and my car broke down about, well, I don't really know how far away, but it sure seemed like a long distance." She took a deep breath and closed her eyes as if willing calm. "Anyway, I'm here now and you're here, thank goodness."

Ethan must have looked confused, and that would make sense because he definitely was. He was glad to help if she was stranded. Perhaps he could call a tow truck for her and let her stay to wait out the storm, but other than that, he wasn't at all sure why she'd been headed this way in the first place.

When she stopped speaking, he took the chance to ask, "Is there something I can do to help you, Miss Leavy?"

"Actually, yes, there is. At least, I hope so."

His heart seemed to speed up as she bit her bottom lip and reached into the pocket of her sweatshirt with both hands. Not that he thought she would pull out a weapon, per se, but because he knew instinctively that nothing she might reveal would be easy to deal with. And what he wanted at that moment, and more than that, for his life in general right then, was just that—simplicity.

But that was simply not in the cards.

So when June Leavy pulled two shivering black-and-white puppies out of her pocket and held them out to show him why she'd driven to his office, walked an unknown distance in a freak snowstorm and nearly pounded down the door, all Ethan Singh could do was sigh.

Chapter Three

As June stared at the junior Dr. Singh awaiting a response, the skin between his brows bunched into a frown over eyes that were cool and impassable, despite what she'd just revealed, making it impossible to determine what he thought of her unannounced arrival on his doorstep. Or rather, *their* arrival.

She knew it was late, that it would be an inconvenience to stop in without even a phone call when the veterinary office had closed over an hour before, but she didn't know what else to do with the two little bundles. She didn't know this man—Ethan, he'd said—but she knew his father, a kind, attentive doctor whose smiles could soothe even the saddest of children when their pets were sick, and for now, that was enough to give her hope that maybe that man's son wouldn't turn her, or her little charges, away on such an awful night.

June hadn't realized she'd been holding her breath until he reached out both hands to take the puppies from her. Letting the air slowly from her lungs, she watched as he tucked them under his arms the same way she had when she'd discovered them in the alley.

"We need to get them warmed up," he said, getting right to business. Ethan turned from where they still stood near the door and lifted a shoulder to motion for her to follow as he headed toward the examination rooms.

June had been in this office many times when her beloved cat reached his twilight years. Being there again caused memories to resurface that she hadn't prepared for when she'd made the impulsive decision to stop in, hoping someone would be there to save two little lives. Trailing behind the doctor, she focused instead on the waves of dark hair that just brushed the collar of his white coat and the broad span of his shoulders. Something about the look of him—the stormy but not unkind dark eyes, the beautiful shade of his skin, like black tea with a bit of milk stirred in, and his height, which had to be considerable to reach well over her own six feet—worked to unravel the tight ball that had formed in her belly.

Driving there in what now seemed to be a full-blast snowstorm was one of the scariest things June had ever done. It was lucky that she knew the roads as well as she did, having lived in Peach Leaf her whole life; otherwise, she wasn't sure there would have been much of a chance of making it this far, not to mention the likelihood that she and the puppies would not have survived if they'd stayed in the car. And until the extreme weather passed, it was impossible to tell what had caused her old lemon to die. Terror had struck when the engine coughed and gave up, the snow coming down so hard as the wind blew fiercely that she could barely see a foot in front of her. She'd followed the road as best she could and somehow, thankfully, had made it to the office.

What was probably only half a mile or so had become a nearly impossible journey until the glass door of the clinic came into view. And now there she was. There hadn't been time to mull over the next step— how she would get home with no working vehicle, especially with the weather throwing such a fit.

At least now she wasn't alone. Even though he didn't seem too happy to see the three of them—and really, who could blame him?—June knew somehow that he would do his best to help. Then they would just have to go from there.

Dr. Singh stopped in front of one of the exam rooms and lifted his chin toward the door, presumably asking June to open it, which she did quickly. When they were all in the room, he held the puppies out to her. "Okay, I need you to hold them for a moment. I'll be right back."

The apprehension she felt must have been poorly hidden because when he saw the look on her face Ethan's stoicism seemed to evaporate briefly; his eyes softened and the thin, serious line of his lips was replaced by a curve at one corner of his mouth that could almost pass for a grin.

"It's okay, Miss Leavy. I'll be right back, I promise. I just need to get some supplies, and it would help if you'd keep the puppies warm for just a moment longer. Can you do that for me?"

June nodded. She'd gotten the babies that far, but the thought of being responsible for them any longer seemed more daunting now as the stress of the day compounded and the idea hit her suddenly that they might not make it. Even now, in the safety of the clinic, with a trained veterinarian to help, the chance remained that the little ones might not pull through.

"Good," he responded, nodding. "You had a great idea earlier, keeping them close together in your pocket. That way, they had each other's warmth, plus that coming from your body."

A little flutter passed through her chest at the mention of her body coming from Dr. Singh's mouth, but she just shook her head and took back the little bundles of fur, tucking them into her sweatshirt once more.

"All set?" he asked.

"Yes, I think so."

At that, he left the room and June concentrated on snuggling the little pups close, willing her warmth to be enough to keep them alive. She couldn't tell how they were doing, other than that the tiny heartbeats she'd felt for before were still thumping softly, and their sweet brown eyes were open. With any luck, that meant they were okay, but a part of her warned that there could be any number of things wrong on the inside.

She swallowed and closed her eyes, and a moment later Dr. Singh returned with what looked like a pile of fluffy towels. He placed the bundle on the exam table and moved to the bench where June sat, wrapping one around her shoulders and gently settling the warm terry cloth in place, a gesture that was completely logical considering that she still shivered from the cold, but also surprisingly intimate. She couldn't recall the last time a man had done something so simple and caring for her, and before she could think about it, she found herself gazing up at him with a warm smile.

"Thank you," she said. "That feels…wonderful."

"You're quite welcome. We've got a small washer and dryer in the staff room, so I warmed these up for a minute or two."

As he spoke, though he didn't exactly return her smile, soft crinkles formed at the outer corners of those deep brown eyes and it struck her just how exceptionally attractive this man was. She hadn't even known that the older Dr. Singh had a son, but then, they'd only shared a doctor/patient-parent relationship, so it made sense that he wouldn't have gone into detail about his family.

Strangely, now, June very much wished he had.

Ethan went back to the table and returned with another towel, kneeling to spread it on the floor at her feet. He sat cross-legged in front of it. "Here, let's put the pups in this while I take a look at them. Safer than having them up on the table for now."

June nodded and retrieved them from her pocket one at a time, cringing as they squeaked in protest at the brief separation. "Do you think…" She swallowed. "Will they be all right?"

"It's hard to know until I can look them over," he said, wrapping the towel around the puppies. "But I will say this." He looked up at her. "You've done a great job here, keeping them warm and bringing them in. From what I can see so far, I think they have a good chance, all because of you."

June's insides melted a little at his compliments, but she wouldn't feel better until she knew the puppies would be okay.

After a few moments, Dr. Singh pulled the towel to one side and very gently moved one puppy closer to him, stroking it softly behind the ears with one hand as he ran his fingers over each tiny limb, probably feeling for broken bones. He then felt the pup's adorable pink tummy, almost grinning when the little guy—she could see plainly now that the term was accurate—closed his eyes.

June placed her nervous hands into the pouch of her hoodie, crossing her fingers.

"It's a good sign that they don't mind being held," Ethan said, using a thumb to gently pry the animal's mouth open, examining its tiny teeth before listening to its heart with the stethoscope that circled his neck. "Their friendliness toward humans will certainly make it easier to place them in homes when the time comes," he pointed out matter-of-factly. "Where did you say you found them?"

June cleared her throat, surprised at how much she disliked talk of giving the puppies away, even though she had no intention of keeping them for herself. "Behind the pizza shop, where I work."

The doctor winced, then looked up and met her eyes, listening intently as she spoke.

"We were done for the day, and I went out to toss the garbage. That's when I found them behind a Dumpster." Her throat threatened to close up as she thought again of someone leaving two little dogs in the icy alley.

"Any idea how long they were there?"

June shook her head. "No. I wish I had more to tell you, but unfortunately, that's it. I didn't know what else to do."

"Well, you did precisely the right thing, though it would appear you endangered yourself attempting to make it here. These are quite the lucky little guys, having been discovered by someone like you. Their fate might have been much worse, as I'm sure I don't have to tell you." An unmistakable wave of sadness crossed over the veterinarian's face.

"I wasn't thinking about that. I just wanted them to be okay…still do."

Ethan nodded and set down the first pup, picking up the other—a girl—to go through the same exam. "There's a good chance they will, thanks to you." Finished, he tucked the brother and sister back into their towel and folded his hands together in his lap.

"So, how's it look?" she asked, nails digging into her palms.

Ethan stared at her, his eyes warmer now, perhaps resigned to the outcome of his evening. She hadn't even considered that he might have plans...perhaps a wife at home waiting for him. Then again, he wasn't wearing a ring and he hadn't texted or called anyone upon her arrival, or once he'd realized that he would be at work for a bit longer.

"Well, I'll have to do some blood work within the next few days to get a full picture, but from what I can tell at this point, it seems they'll be okay."

Relief flooded through her at the optimistic statement.

"They're about three and a half weeks old, give or take. No broken bones, healthy lungs and hearts, and their teeth are coming in, which is great news."

"So they can eat solid food? We won't have to feed them with a bottle?" June had to admit she was a little disappointed. The idea of holding the tiny puppies and feeding them sounded...nice. She had always wanted children, anyway, but after her experience with Clayton, she wasn't sure she could trust anyone enough ever again to even think about building a life with another person. Another person who had the potential to break her heart. Maybe someday, if she ever had the time and energy to spare, she could have a little puppy just like these to care for. Maybe she could try letting herself love something again... one day...but it would take time, far more than she could spare with her life the way it was, working sixty-hour weeks at the pizza parlor just to pay her rent and keep her car in working shape. She hoped things wouldn't be that way forever; it was a sobering thought.

"Yes, they can eat solid food, but we'll need to mix it with some canine milk replacer that's specially formulated for puppies. Cow's or any other kind of milk would upset their tummies."

For some reason, June grinned at the word, so much more fatherly and sweet than the more technical *stomachs*.

"Do you have that here?"

"Sure do. We've got plenty, and I can have my receptionist, Sadie, order more in the morning if need be." He lifted a corner of the towel and glanced in at the puppies. "For now, we need to get them some water and get a little food in them. We won't give them too much yet, as I don't know what or how much they've been eating and I don't want them to get bloated."

June nodded as he stood and held out a hand to help her do the same, then knelt to pick up the squeaky bundle. He led her to the back area and into a room lined with shelves of food and medicine, handing over the puppies so he could scan the stock for what they needed.

"Ah, here we are," he said, lifting a small bag from a top shelf.

He opened a cabinet and pulled out two shallow bowls, then headed to the back room, stopping at a sink to fill one with water. Into the other, he poured a small amount of pebble-size kibble. He grabbed a bottle from a nearby refrigerator and poured thin, white liquid on top, like milk on cereal. Placing the bowls on the floor in a corner, Ethan motioned for June to set down the towel. At the scent of the food, two little black noses began to wriggle and both humans laughed quietly.

"The little stinkers are cute, aren't they?"

Ethan looked up at her as he spoke and this time his smile reached those gorgeous, mahogany eyes. She felt his gaze all the way down into her middle, as warm and comforting as the towel he'd so recently wrapped around her shoulders.

"Very," she replied, her voice little more than the squeaky sound the puppies made.

Dr. Singh helped her to guide the puppies over to the bowls, and they watched with bated breath, waiting to see if the little ones would eat. Finally, both pups sniffed at the bowl of food and buried their faces in the kibble, and the sound of Ethan's and June's sighs of relief were audible.

As the dogs worked on their dinner, Ethan disappeared into the supply closet and returned holding what looked like a baby gate and paper towels. He set to work in the corner of the room, spreading out what June now saw were puppy pads, which he surrounded with the gate, creating a little pen. "All right. We'll settle them in here for a bit, give them a little time and see if they'll do their business, then we can put them to bed."

He looked up at June. "If I'm correct on their

age, they should be able to go to the bathroom on their own."

"What do you mean?"

"Well, if they're too young, they'll need a little help to go, but I'm hoping they're old enough." He winked at her. "Time will tell."

"Ah." June had never been around such young animals before; once again, she was thankful to have an ally who knew far more than she about this unexpected development in her evening.

"In the meantime, is there anything I can get you?"

Her stomach grumbled, reminding her that she hadn't yet eaten and it was almost nine o'clock, but she doubted there was much in the way of people food in a veterinary clinic. "I'd love something hot to drink. That is, if you have anything."

"Come," Dr. Singh said, holding out an arm. June walked through the door in front of him and he left it open, leading her to what had to be the staff break room, where he pulled a chair from a small, round table, motioning for her to sit.

She watched as he took a measuring cup from a cabinet and placed it on a hot plate before pulling milk from the fridge and what appeared to be a few spice bottles from a drawer.

"So tell me, Miss Leavy…"

"Please, call me June."

He set to work, mixing ingredients in the glass cup as though he were a chef in an upscale kitchen, rather than a very patient veterinarian in a small-town clinic. "June, then. Have you ever had chai?"

It was only one of her favorite drinks. "Oh, I love chai tea."

The doctor let out a chuckle as he stirred the mixture with a spoon.

"What's so funny?"

"Just chai. When you say *chai tea*, what you're really saying is *tea tea*. The word *chai* means *tea* in Hindi."

"Oh, goodness," she said, feeling like a doofus. "I'm sorry."

"Not at all," Ethan said, laughing.

June found she very much liked the deep, warm sound of it tickling her ears. He seemed much more relaxed now than he had when she'd first arrived, almost certainly ruining his night.

"Is your family from India?" she asked, surprising herself. She supposed it wouldn't hurt to find something to talk about to pass the time until the storm let up and she could go on home.

"My father was born in Delhi and came here as a child."

"And your mother?"

"She's American, from New York. They've lived in Texas for most of my life, since my father opened this clinic."

It was quiet for a few moments as Ethan continued to stir the tea and June took a couple of deep breaths, allowing herself to calm down for the first time since she'd found the puppies over two hours ago. Her shoulders ached with tension and her tiredness reached all the way down to her bones; she longed for a hot shower and her bed. For once, she would be happy to go home to her lonely, closet-size apartment, where she hoped to get at least a couple hours of sleep before her alarm clock sent her back to work.

When she opened her eyes, Ethan set two steaming mugs on the table and June lifted hers to take a sip. The hot liquid soaked all the way down into her veins, warming her through and through, the sweet, yet spicy, flavors tingling her throat in an incredibly pleasant way. "Oh, my gosh," she said, rolling her eyes toward the roof, "this is amazing."

Ethan grinned, then took a sip from his own mug. "Better than Starbucks, huh?"

"Um, yeah. Way better. Apples and oranges better."

"I'm glad you like it," he said, taking a few more sips. He got up and went back to the counter, turning on a small television set to the same local weather she'd watched earlier with Margaret. She made a mental note to text her boss soon to make sure she'd made it home.

"We'd better see what's going on out there," he said, returning to the table. "It looked much worse than I thought it was when I opened the door and you brought an arctic blast in with you and those puppies."

"It's pretty bad. I'm hoping it will clear so I can get home soon."

Ethan looked skeptical but didn't say anything as they both turned to watch the screen. It only took a few minutes for them to learn that the weather had gotten worse as they'd been taking care of the dogs. According to the meteorologist, a mass of cold, dry Canadian air had moved south into their area to intersect with a warm, moist air mass moving north from the Gulf of Mexico. Evidently, the cold air had advanced and pushed away the warm air, orchestrating the crazy mess outside. Over a foot of snow had fallen on already-icy roads and the whole of Peach Leaf was now under a winter weather warning.

June put her elbows on the table and lowered her head into her arms. It would be hours before it would be safe to drive home...for a person who had a working ride.

"Well, June," Ethan said, getting up to turn off the steady stream of impending doom on the television. "Looks like you're stuck with me for a while."

"I... I can't stay here. I've got to get home."

Ethan tilted his head. "Not going to happen, at least not tonight. It's really nasty out there—not anywhere close to safe for driving." He finished the last of his tea and picked up both of their cups, carrying them to the sink.

"My car's broken down, anyway. Surely I can at least get a tow truck out here. Maybe they can take me home."

Ethan came back and sat down across from her at the table. "It's not likely we'd be able to get a tow truck out here in this weather. I would drive you if I felt it was safe, but I've spent some time in Alaska and I've seen firsthand what can happen when people don't heed weather warnings." He paused, perhaps not wishing to sound overly concerned. "Of course, I'm not going to stop you from leaving, June, but I have to tell you, I don't think it's safe, and I'd really rather you not put yourself into any more danger than you already have today."

Ignoring the fact that this man shouldn't care about her well-being so much, June ran through all of her options in her head—all zero of them. She sighed. He was right. She was stuck there for the foreseeable future. She'd never in her life experienced such a dangerous storm and she definitely didn't know how to safely travel in one. Besides, she had the puppies to think of now. The minute she'd picked them up, they'd become her responsibility, and she couldn't just abandon them with a doctor who had other patients to care for, especially one who was only temporarily managing his father's clinic.

She looked up at Dr. Singh, who appeared almost as uneasy as she.

"I hate to break it to you, June, but under the circumstances, the smartest thing for you to do is to spend the night here with me."

Chapter Four

It took June longer than it should have to register what Dr. Singh—Ethan—had said. Mostly because, somehow, she'd gotten momentarily lost in those cinnamon eyes of his. The man was handsome in a way that could almost be described as beautiful, but his looks were also sort of unnerving at the same time, as though they had the potential power to unravel her completely.

It occurred to her that looks like his didn't really fit in with the men she was used to seeing in Peach Leaf, almost as though she'd woken up still inside a dream involving a movie set. Men who looked like Ethan Singh were generally employed as actors or male models...not small-town veterinarians. And they usually associated with other exceptionally attractive or powerful people, or in his case, highly educated people…people nothing like her.

Staring at him made her think of all the ways she couldn't quite measure up. Though she wasn't sure where that notion had even originated from. After all, why would she need to measure up at all?

It wasn't like he was interested in her, at least aside from his medical duty to assist her in getting the puppies healthy. He certainly wasn't interested in her as a woman, as well he shouldn't be, because she was not interested in him as a man.

Really, she was not.

She shouldn't be, at any rate, not after what she'd been through the past several months. No woman in her right mind would seek to get back out there after the burn she'd suffered. And even though she might not be thinking clearly, what with her only real possession stuck out in the snow enduring God only knew what horrors, which might prevent it from ever working again—and with this man staring at her with unmistakable amusement as she waited for appropriate words to arrive—she could at least be certain that she was, in fact, in her right mind.

With that, she cleared the cobwebs from her throat and finally spoke, hoping her voice wouldn't come out too rusty from lack of use.

"Um, okay. I guess that makes sense." She swiped a hand across her forehead, suddenly warm despite the weather outside and the room's cool temperature.

"Of course it does," Ethan answered, his tone final as if the issue had been decided and there was nothing more to be discussed. But June thought there was plenty in need of discussion. Like, for example, the fact that she was suddenly starving.

And not, it would seem as she found herself in danger of falling deep into those eyes again, just for food.

The thought rushed in unbidden and was stuck there in her mind before she could stop it, meaning that the mature thing now would be to address where it had come from and what it meant. At some point. For now, feeling more ragged than she did after a double shift at work and hungrier than she could ever recall having been before, maturity was the last thing on her mind.

"Is something wrong?" the devastatingly handsome doctor asked, his voice even sexier thanks to its thick note of concern.

June shook her head. "No, it's fine. Or in any case, I suppose it has to be." She looked away from him and, not surprisingly, her mind was instantly clearer.

She would have to be careful around those eyes from now on, especially if she was meant to endure an entire night—possibly more, if the weather didn't clear up—with a man who looked like he'd just walked out of the latest glossy issue of *GQ*.

He made her want things she shouldn't want, things she couldn't have.

"What is it, then?"

When she didn't answer, he tilted his head like a curious puppy—like a ridiculously adorable, curious puppy.

"Come on now, I can tell you were thinking about something."

Like a tickle of wind against her cheek, she sensed him staring at her, willing her to speak.

"It's just that, well—" a hand flew to her stomach involuntarily "—I'm starving."

Ethan threw his head back and laughed, the sound low and sultry and full of mischief, leaving June almost frustrated with his level of physical perfection. Couldn't he at least have an absurd-sounding, high-pitched laugh or something? Was there nothing about this guy that wouldn't make her want to kiss him?

It was just her luck—she should be used to this by now—to be stuck overnight with the most distractingly attractive guy she'd ever met, right after the absolute worst breakup she'd ever endured.

Come on, Junie, she chastised herself. *That's about enough negativity for two lifetimes, don't you think?*

Best to push on. Besides, with the cards she'd been dealt, what choice did she have?

"All right. What's so darn funny?" she asked.

"Nothing, really. It's just that here you are looking so incredibly serious and come to find out you're just hungry."

"Hilarious," she responded, this time allowing a hint of playfulness to escape. "But seriously, I haven't had anything to eat since lunch, which now seems like years ago. I know it might be useless to ask, but is there anything to eat around here? That is, anything we can get to without risking our lives."

Ethan grinned, his full lips setting in motion a series of thoughts that she wasn't entirely certain were legal.

"Actually, this might be one problem we can solve."

"Don't tease me now. I'm this close to sneaking some of that puppy kibble from the storage room."

He laughed. "I wouldn't dare. There's a bakery a few doors down. It might be a rough trip, but I think if we stay right next to the building and, well, right next to each other, we can probably make it with only minimal danger."

"Stay—" June swallowed "—next to each other?"

"Of course. For warmth."

June felt her cheeks heat, hoping they weren't turning as ghastly pink as they were in the habit of doing—the eternal curse of redheads like herself. "Yes, right. Warmth. Of course."

It made perfect sense under the circumstances; it really did. But the mere thought of being near Ethan for the duration it might take them to reach sustenance raised her temperature enough that she was fairly certain she could comfortably walk all the way to her apartment in the wind that had begun to howl outside the clinic like a wild animal.

Without a coat.

"Let's check on the puppies, get you bundled back up and see if we can't get some food," Ethan said, tossing his new companion a sweet smile. "I could go for some dinner myself."

While that was definitely true—his stomach had been protesting against its emptiness since he'd seen his last patient, and that had been hours ago—there was another reason, equal in weight to the first, that he'd suggested leaving the office and grabbing something to eat.

That reason was June Leavy.

A few hours before, his life in Peach Leaf had been simple and clear, intentionally so.

This morning, he'd woken with a relatively muddled head for the first time since leaving Colorado.

Since he'd left *her*.

Sure, he still thought about his ex a few times a day still; that was perfectly normal following the demise of a serious relationship. But aside from those few painful moments, things had actually started to look up, and he'd gotten into a comfortable groove. Wake up and go for an early run, shower and eat breakfast, arrive at the clinic before sunrise to relieve the night technician and check on the overnight patients, work through his father's back-to-back appointments, breaking only for a quick lunch, and then go home after he'd completed evening rounds and closed up. He'd say goodbye to the staff and head home, too tired to think. Working from dark sky to dark sky suited him at this odd juncture in his life. The routine kept him busy and, most importantly, left little time for ruminating over all he'd left behind.

At least it had, until that evening, when June Leavy had burst through the door, literally bringing with her a blast of fresh air.

The image made him smile. As cold as it had been when she'd walked in, June was about as different from his frosty ex as she could be—a truth he didn't really want to examine closely.

But as beautiful as June was, as sweet and warm as he could clearly see she was even in the limited time they'd spent together, the truth remained that her presence was simply not welcome.

She filled the room in a way that, while extremely pleasant—intoxicating, even—made him uncomfortable. Tall, bright in color and in mood and lively, June was impossible to ignore. Sharing a cup of tea with her had been difficult enough, but offering to let her stay the night—something he'd had no choice but to do on account of the growing danger outside—was going to take an iron will.

He didn't want her in his clinic, didn't want her on his mind. Being in the same room with her for the past while, as warm as she made him feel, he'd almost forgotten about the blizzard wailing away outside.

All of which was dangerous. What he needed was space, and a clear head.

Taking June for a bite to eat was the perfect solution. They were both hungry, and it would give him a chance to get a grip on whatever spark she'd ignited within him. Plus, he'd like to check on his father's business neighbors—the couple who owned the German bakery next door had been there for years and were close with his dad. They were elderly, and it would be good to make sure they were holding up through the freak snowstorm.

A blast of frigid air would do him good, and then he could figure out how to handle himself around June for the rest of the evening.

Things came to mind. So many things.

None of them realistic, or even appropriate for that matter.

A guy like him was in no position to be picturing those endless legs curled up next to his on the office sofa, for example, or better yet, wrapped around his middle as he kissed the daylights out of those undoubtedly soft lips and…

No. He couldn't let himself go there. Not again. It was stupid enough that he'd allowed his thoughts to wander this far. It seemed any time he ventured away from work for five minutes, he landed in trouble. He didn't want to be the sort of man who was so easily distracted by a pretty face and a pair of killer legs.

He looked up to find the object of his musings worrying her bottom lip as she studied him.

It wasn't sexy, the way she did that. Not at all.

The resultant swelling of those soft pink clouds did not affect him. Not in the least.

Also, he needed to check the thermostat—had it gotten warmer inside the clinic?

"So, what kind of place is it?" June asked, her cheeks slightly more flushed than they'd been when she first came in from the wind. Surely she wasn't… she couldn't possibly be having similar thoughts to the ones he'd been entertaining. The idea was absurd.

He'd been radiating a cool demeanor and a general
leave me alone, I'm busy attitude for weeks now
that would put off any woman. More likely, she was
just in a hurry to get out of there as much as he was.

"I mean what kind of food do they have?"

"Oh, well, there's the rub," he answered, trying not
to get distracted again by those wicked lips, which
had reddened to a pretty ruby shade—from the cold
or from her nibbling, he no longer cared.

And what difference did it make, anyway?

It certainly didn't matter that they looked good
enough to feast on himself, like fresh cherries ripe
for the picking.

Dammit!

What the hell had they been talking about again?

"The rub?"

Ah, yes.

"It's just a little German bakery, you see. So we
won't be able to get any real dinner. We'll have to
skip straight to dessert. Hopefully it'll do until the
weather lets up and you have a chance to head on
your way." A thought that disturbed him far more
than he cared to acknowledge.

Something crossed her features very briefly—a
shadowy hint of darkness, perhaps—and then disappeared.

Was it something he'd said that had so quickly
stolen the light from her eyes?

He didn't have time to figure it out before she
spoke again.

"Oh, that's right. How silly of me to forget. I've

been working such weird hours the past few years that I haven't been to Bauer's in ages—I'd forgotten about the place until now." Her features softened into wistfulness. "My mom used to take me there as a kid, on special occasions. They have the best pastry and…"

She blushed again and he wished to touch the crimson apples on her cheeks. He enjoyed her rambling—quite a lot actually. But what good would it do to say so? After that night, she would be gone and he would go back to his temporary, if somewhat lonely, life.

Still, it was nice to see her talk about something so obviously important to her; it was nice to see inside her just a little.

"Anyway, I'm rambling, but that will be just fine. I'm so hungry I really don't care what we eat, as long as it passes for food."

"And is preferably intended for human consumption," he teased, recalling her earlier comment about kibble, and wanting to restore her brightness.

"That would be great," she said, beaming.

Pleased, he gestured for her to follow him to the back room and she did so. When they stepped through the door, the puppies were curled so tightly together that he and June had to check to make sure the little ones were both accounted for. After changing out the potty pad, they watched the critters sleep for a few moments, Ethan checking their breathing before he gently touched June's elbow, whispered that the pups would be okay with only each other as company for a short while longer and led her out to the front of the clinic.

"I feel like I'm leaving my kids alone at home," June said, shrugging into her coat, which he held open for her.

"I completely understand, and sadly, I don't think this is their first time on their own," Ethan said, wanting to reassure her, "but we won't be long and I promise they'll be fine until we return."

What was he thinking, making a promise like that? Yes, the animals appeared relatively healthy and strong, considering their situation, and yes, he was confident in his ability to usher them back to full health, but he had no history of clairvoyance and therefore no business making guarantees regarding things he couldn't fully control.

What had gotten into him? Would he say anything to make this woman smile?

Catching the worried crease between her brows as she glanced once more over her shoulder in the direction of the pups, Ethan tucked his hand beneath her elbow. "Trust me, June. They'll be all right. Their bellies are full, they've had fresh water and have done their business, they're safe inside the pen and they're not alone."

The answer was yes, apparently, he would say anything.

At his words, her expression softened, and though he didn't want to examine why it mattered to him at all, he found himself relieved at the idea of having provided some comfort. "Also, I would not leave them if I believed them to be unsafe, okay?"

She nodded.

"So then, do you trust me?"

She wasn't quick to answer, a fact that made him like her even more. After all—though he wasn't entirely sure any longer whether he believed time to be a reliable factor in the decision to invest trust in someone—they'd only known each other for little over an hour.

"Yes," she finally said. "I do trust you."

He smiled, more pleased than wisdom should allow.

"Good." He squeezed her elbow, then let go. "I figure the best thing to do now is grab something to go and come back here. That way, we won't risk getting stuck at the bakery. Even though it's only a few yards away, we could end up unable to get back, and I don't want to leave the puppies alone for a full night."

"Sounds like a plan," June agreed.

Ethan pulled on his coat and wrapped a scarf around his neck and face before donning his hat. By the time he'd finished, June had done the same and looked adorable, a description that, despite being worlds apart from characterizing the women he was typically attracted to, seemed somehow more enticing.

June looked like someone he could curl up and have hot chocolate with after a long day at work, someone who would be joyful when a guy walked in the door, happy to spend an evening at home with him just relaxing, doing nothing in particular.

That was just it—the sight of her evoked *home* to him, something he could never ascribe to the women he'd dated before, women who preferred nights out on the town on the arm of a successful professor. It didn't escape him that, over the past few years, being a "nerd" had become an asset, one he'd not hesitated to take full advantage of, and there had been plenty of young women, even a few former students, who had been eager to date an up-and-coming scientist who'd begun, much to his dismay, to attract media attention.

But June was part of a different world than the one he'd become accustomed to. For reasons he couldn't explain, she brought to mind everything he missed about living in a small town, being close to family and so much more. He'd spent a good portion of the last decade thinking only of his career, dedicating all of his time to furthering his research and, if he was honest, to impressing his department at the university.

June made him think of other things. Things he used to want but truly thought he didn't need any longer—things like home, and family, and someone to share it with. Someone to love.

None of which he would entertain, because that word—*love*—was no longer part of his vocabulary when it came to women.

Of course he loved his parents, his siblings and his nieces and nephews, but that was the safe kind of love. Loving a woman, which would inevitably lead to a broken heart again—well, that was an experience he'd rather not repeat. Especially not when his heart hadn't quite healed from the last.

What kind of scientist would he be if he didn't learn from failed experiments?

"Remind me again why we're doing this?" June asked as he opened the door and snow crashed through with the force of a speeding train.

He reached for her hand and, when she grabbed it with her own, pulled her close to his body, tucking an arm over her shoulders. He chose to ignore the way she stiffened as their figures came together, not caring to assess whether it was aversion or pleasure at the contact that made her react in such a way.

"Because we're starving, remember?"

"Oh, right," she said. "Somehow the idea of having my face frozen off made me forget how hungry I am."

He started to laugh but stopped when icy air hit his lungs, and set his focus on moving ahead instead. As they made their way in the direction of the bakery, Ethan was careful to keep his free hand against the wall of the building as the wind's forceful blasts threatened to send them flying into the white abyss that used to be a parking lot. June's head was down, her chin tucked into the top of her coat as he led the way. Despite the circumstances, Ethan couldn't help but enjoy the way her tall, slim figure nestled against his own, her body's warmth seeping through the layers of his clothing, strong enough to set off a flame in his lower abdomen.

Astounding, the lack of discipline he'd allowed in letting himself get carried away over June. Having her huddle against his skin for warmth was one thing; that just made practical, biological sense.

Letting her under it, though, was another matter entirely.

"Looks like there's a note on the door," Ethan shouted to June, who was still tucked under his arm. It was virtually impossible to hear himself think, let alone to communicate with each other with the high-speed wind whipping around them. They were only a couple of yards from Bauer's Bakery and, Ethan hoped, his stomach growling like an angry dog, something hot to eat.

He felt June nod beneath his shoulder as it occurred to him for the first time, stupidly, that the Bauers might have closed up early and hit the road once the weather started to get worse. He certainly couldn't blame them; it's exactly what he would have done if he didn't have so many little furry creatures depending on him. Even if he'd been able to earlier before June showed up, after he'd told the overnight tech not to risk the trip in, he would never have left the babies alone on a night like this.

As soon as they made it to the door of the bakeshop, June emerged from his side and reached for it, only to find it locked. He wasn't surprised, but he sure as hell was disappointed. The note on the door had been taped at all four corners, three of which were now torn. Peeling off the last, he read it only to confirm his earlier assumption that the Bauers had gone home, and he was glad for their safety.

"Well, crap," June said, turning to face him. "Guess we'll have to head back to the clinic. Maybe we can find a granola bar to split or something. Or… doggy biscuits are basically flour and water, right? So, maybe if we use our imaginations, it would be like eating cookies."

He'd have to be a little more desperate to try a canine treat, but if they did find a granola bar, Ethan would let June have the whole thing. However, it was too early in the game to consider giving up just yet.

"Hang on a minute."

June's face was bright pink from the well-below-freezing temperature and the wind's icy fingers slapping at her cheeks. He needed to get her inside that building, needed to get her warm.

"I've got a key." He took off one mitten and, reaching under his coat, pulled his wallet out of his back pocket and dug through the compartments until he found what he was looking for. "My dad gave it to me in case the Bauers had an emergency."

June didn't look too relieved; probably she was holding out to make sure it worked. That made two of them. He hadn't paid much attention when Dad went through all the important numbers and files and such that Ethan might need while caring for the clinic, and it hadn't occurred to him to check and see if the key worked. Who would have guessed that the worst storm in Texas history would hit during his stay?

"Well, what are you waiting for?" she yelled so he could hear, her eyes squinting against the brutal air.

With fingers on the brink of frostbite, he gripped the key and shoved it into the lock, releasing an audible sigh when it fit and the knob turned.

"Oh, thank God," June said, her eyes shooting toward the sky.

Ethan opened the door and ushered her inside, pulling it closed against a turbulent gust.

Once inside, Ethan leaned his back against the door, then they looked at each other and both started laughing as relief and the possibility of getting their hands on some food settled in. The moment of relaxation didn't last long, though, and suddenly Ethan heard a sharp, incessant beeping.

"Oh, crap!" he shouted, echoing June's words from when she'd thought they were locked out in the cold. This could be worse.

When she met his eyes, hers were wide as salad plates. "Is that what I think it is?"

"Uh, yeah. 'Fraid so."

"Oh, no. No, no, no." Her hands flew to her cheeks and she stared at him with obvious fear. "We are going to be in so much trouble when the police..."

He held up a hand in an attempt to prevent her panic from gaining momentum.

"Hang on. It would take them ages to get here if they were coming at all, but I've got a strong feeling that's not going to happen. Luckily, I also have a plan." He reached into his pocket once more, praying his phone was still in there; he hadn't checked before they left the clinic, a distraction he could justifiably blame on June. He pressed his thumb against a button, unlocking the cell, and dialed as quickly as his icicle fingers would allow.

"What are you doing?"

"Just trust me, okay?"

She nodded at the same time his father picked up.

"Dad, hey, I'm glad you answered. I need you to listen carefully. I don't have much time."

"Ethan, is that you?" his father asked.

He rolled his eyes.

"Yes, Dad, of course it's me. Look, do you have the alarm code to the Bauers' place?"

He waved at June to get her attention and motioned for her to open the keypad near the door where the alarm continued to blare its warning.

"Just a minute, son, I think I have it here somewhere." Ethan could picture the older man digging through the kitchen junk drawer of his uncle's apartment in DC.

Ethan groaned—getting his father to hurry up was about as futile as trying to force a cat to walk on a leash—but thankfully, he'd set to work without an argument.

"Time is of the essence here, Dad."

"All right, all right. I've got it right in front of me now. Just let me put on my reading glasses." More shuffling ensued. "Are you ready?"

"Of course I am. Go ahead."

He listened as his dad recited the code, repeating it to June, who promptly punched the numbers into the keypad. When the inane beeping stopped, Ethan dropped the phone to his side and they both let out the breaths they'd been holding since the noise began.

"Is everything okay now?" his father's voice chimed from the cell.

"Yes, Dad, it's fine. Thanks a bunch. It's a long story and I can't talk now, but I needed to get into the Bauers' and I've got the key you gave me. I just hadn't considered the alarm system."

"Tell Dr. Singh thank you for me," June called out.

He nodded that he would.

"Is that a girl?" his dad asked.

Ethan rolled his eyes. "Yes, Dad. And she said to tell you she's thankful for the help, as well. But like I said, I'll have to explain later. I have to go…"

"What girl?" came his mother's voice in the background.

Grumbling rose up from his throat when he heard her snatch the phone from his father's hand.

Here we go.

"Ethan Singh, do you have a girlfriend you haven't told us about? Are you on a date? You should not be on the phone while on a date. I raised you better than that and…"

"Mom, Mom! I'm not on a date." He shook his head at the curious, teasing smile that sprung up on June's face. She crossed her arms, clearly enjoying his misery just a little too much.

"Look, like I told Dad, I've got to go. I'll talk to you guys later."

"You'd better not be out with a woman and keeping it a secret from us, Ethan. I'm your mother and I deserve to know if your heart isn't broken anymore and you're back out there. Are you back out there, Ethan? I certainly hope so. I never liked that last girl and I know you can do so much better."

"Jessica, Mom. Her name was Jessica. All right, thanks for the lecture. I really do have to go, though."

"Bring her by the house so we can meet her, son," his dad interjected from the background. "I don't know if your mother has told you yet but we're coming back down for Neena's birthday party in a few days. We will see your new friend then."

"Yes, do so," Melanie Singh agreed. "And sooner rather than later. I don't like to see you so down all the time."

He could practically see the maternal finger shaking in his face.

"You're not getting any younger, Ethan," she continued, "and I want to see you settled before you're old and gray."

He gazed heavenward, hoping maybe the guy upstairs would throw him a bone. As if getting stuck in a blizzard without dinner wasn't bad enough, now he had to endure an inquisition from his overinvolved parents while a woman he'd been attracted to the moment he laid eyes on her looked on with thinly veiled amusement.

June could at least have the courtesy not to look so thoroughly entertained.

"Yes, Mom. Tell Dad I said bye. I will talk to you later."

"Not so fast. First, promise you'll bring this young lady by for Neena's birthday party. The more, the merrier, I always say."

He'd never heard her use that expression before in his life, but this was a time for picking battles.

"I can't do that."

"And why ever not?"

His jaw clenched and he withheld choice words. "Because as I said, we are not dating. If you'd been listening you would know that we've only just met, June and I. Now I really do have to go."

"Oh, June is such a pretty name, but, Ethan, if you're not dating this young woman, then what are you doing with her in the middle of this weather? After the clinic is closed?"

"She's not...we're not..." He closed his eyes, drawing in a slow breath and hopefully a hefty dose of patience, too. "I will explain later."

"I know you, Ethan," his mother said, her voice stern now. "The party. Next weekend. You'll call me later for the details."

"I..." Oh, what was the point in fighting her? When Melanie Singh got an idea in her head, there was simply no talking her out of it. "All right, Mom. I promise."

"Good boy," she said, the sound of victory clear as a bell in her falsely innocent voice.

He knew when to admit defeat. "Okay, Mom. Goodbye."

He pushed the end call button with a bit more ferocity than was necessary. June was standing there staring at him, arms still crossed, a pleased grin curling her lips up at the corners.

"You don't have to look so smug, you know."

June's eyebrows shot up. "Smug?" she asked, pointing at her chest. "Who, me?"

She batted her eyelashes, a gesture that was meant to be silly but instead ticked up his pulse a notch.

"Yes, smug. I can see you got a kick out of watching me get dominated by my overbearing family, and you're enjoying it far too much." He shoved his cell back into his pocket and took a few steps nearer to the woman who'd turned his evening upside down— whether in a good way or bad still remained to be seen.

Something in her eyes darkened, but she quickly brushed aside whatever had bothered her for half a second. "Not at all. I mean, I did enjoy listening in on your conversation, I admit, but probably not in the way you think."

"I'm intrigued. Go on." It was his turn to cross his arms, and he did so with a smile on his face, enjoying the easy banter with her. It had been a long time since he'd felt so tranquil in a woman's presence, and even though he wasn't willing to invest his heart in one again, what harm could there be in having a bit of fun? They were stuck in each other's company for the night, after all. Maybe it wouldn't hurt to enjoy the short time they had.

He expected June's next words to be playful, flirty even, but instead they were serious.

"It's just that…well, it sounds like your parents are very sweet. You're a lucky guy."

"Oh, June, you have no idea," he said softly, trying to set the tone to light again. "My parents are many things, but sweet is not one of them."

Her eyes crinkled at the corners and registered disbelief. "You're bluffing. They sound incredibly sweet."

"They are kind people, I'll allow that. But—" he made a clicking sound with his tongue "—meddlesome to an unholy degree."

He stood only inches away from her now, and the heat radiating in that small space was enough to warm the entire cold bakery.

"At any rate, I'm in debt to them for that alarm code, so I'm in no position to complain."

"Goodness, me, too," June added. "I think my butt was literally about to freeze off."

"Wouldn't that be a shame?" he quipped, the words popping out before he could reconsider.

June would have been justified in socking him a good one, but the thing was, he didn't for a second regret the comment. It was true—the woman had a great ass—and he wasn't afraid to admit it.

For a second, her pretty mouth hung open in surprise, and then it did something rather unexpected.

She smiled—a gorgeous, sexy smile—even a little naughty, he would say, and he couldn't help but grin back.

They stood there like two teenage idiots on a first

date until finally June gave a little cough. "Right. Food," he said, more than a little sorry to see the moment pass.

Chapter Five

"Obviously no one's here, so what are we going to do?"

Ethan pulled off his outerwear and made a motion for June to let him help with her coat. He plucked the garment from her shoulders and she was instantly grateful for the air that slid over her skin like cool water.

He'd gone and done it again—made her uncomfortably warm with that silky voice and those delicious brown eyes. Not to mention she was certain her heart would melt as she'd listened to his humorous but charming conversation with his folks.

June swallowed, willing the lump in her throat to dissolve.

She loved her own mom fiercely, but that had

never stopped her from wanting more as a kid, from wanting a real family. A whole family. It was easy to admit that she wasn't a kid anymore, that she should grow up and accept reality, but some wishes did not go away.

When her ex had deceived her, stolen every cent of the money she'd saved to start her own bakery, then topped that off by leaving her in the dust with a shattered heart, she'd thought more than once how comforting it would have been to have a sister. And yeah, she had good friends—not many that she kept in touch with, considering the long hours her job required, but a few close ones nonetheless. Her best friend, Katie, was always there for her, when she and her husband, Ryan, weren't too busy with their kids' many activities. It was just that sometimes she couldn't help thinking how wonderful it would be to have someone she'd grown up with, someone who knew her history—who loved her deeply and unconditionally—to have her back when things got really tough. Really, really tough. Like you're-on-your-back-and-someone-kicks-you-in-the-face kind of tough. That's certainly how she'd felt when Clayton had taken everything she'd ever invested into the bakery.

And, it sometimes seemed, much more.

On the loneliest nights in her tiny apartment, without even a cat to keep her company anymore, June sometimes felt like he'd taken her very future from her. To her name, she had a rented apartment, a car she didn't yet own and a job that paid only slightly over minimum wage. Nothing that really, truly, belonged to her.

Sometimes her whole life felt borrowed, as if someone could come collect at any time and she would have nothing left but the clothes on her back.

Of course, she would never admit that to anyone—not ever. She was June Leavy, the positive girl who'd grown up poor with a single mom who broke her back at multiple jobs to put food on the table but could never scrape together enough for a much-deserved vacation—all with a smile on her face.

Because if she didn't smile, there was only one alternative. And even on her lowest days, feeling sorry for herself was not an option.

And then there was Ethan Singh, saving puppies and rocking her world during the biggest storm of her life.

If she didn't watch herself, he might convince her that she was not a woman who no longer trusted men. Or, at least, he might make her want to try.

She gave herself a mental shake.

No way. She wasn't going there again. She knew to stay away from a face like that when she saw one. Her ex had been a good-looking guy and she'd been the envy of all her friends, until he'd broken her heart into a thousand little pieces.

She was a much stronger woman now, and would not fall victim to a handsome face, liquid-gold voice and a knock-your-pants-off body.

"We're going to do what we came to do—get something to eat."

His comment brought her back to the present situation. She was starving, yes, but she wasn't about to steal food from a sweet old couple who'd pinched her cheeks as a child. Perhaps they could leave a note and pay later.

"We can't just take food when no one's here."

"Of course we can. These are dire circumstances, June, on the off chance you haven't noticed."

Something about the way he said her name turned her insides into custard.

"I've known the Bauers since my dad opened the clinic, and they won't mind one bit."

She was skeptical and it must have shown in her expression.

"Look, there's nothing to worry about. I'll leave a note and some cash and drop by to explain when the storm is over. No worries. Besides, I'm pretty sure Mrs. Bauer would hate to see us leave here empty-handed. She's always bringing the clinic staff cookies and trying to fatten us up. If anything, she'll be happy we helped ourselves."

He had a point there. The Bauers were childless and seemed to take immense joy in spoiling other peoples' kids with their stellar baked goods. The bakery was their passion and the older couple loved nothing more than watching people savor their home-made desserts.

She wasn't exactly keen on the idea, but desperate times and all...

"If you're sure."

Ethan pulled a large bill out of his wallet and left

it on the counter, promising to find a pen and paper before they left.

"I'm sure."

She raised her hands in surrender. "I suppose we don't really have a choice, now do we?"

"That's my girl."

The words hit her harder than the wind outside. Why did she like them so much? And why, when she'd only been around him for a few hours, did this guy have the power to unravel her with a couple of words?

Yep, she definitely needed to watch out.

As if to remind her that biology had a say in things, June's stomach let out a lion-worthy roar, making Ethan laugh and lightening the mood.

She covered her mouth to stifle a grin. "Sorry about that."

"Nonsense. Let's just get something in there already."

"Deal."

With that, they made their way behind the glass cases, which had been emptied for the night, and into the kitchen. June didn't see any pastries, but the scent of fresh dough tickled her nose and made her even hungrier, if such a thing was possible at that point. And yet there was absolutely no food in sight. Which made perfect sense—under normal circumstances, the Bauers would be there early in the morning to make everything from scratch for the day. Unfortunately, there were two ravenous people in need of immediate sustenance, and baked goods weren't exactly known for being made quickly.

Ethan appeared as disappointed as she felt.

"Okay, so I don't see anything to eat, and now's probably as good a time as any to admit that I know less than nothing about baking."

June chuckled, scanning the shelves stocked with flour, sugar and other products. She had an idea that just might work if she could drum up the right stuff. "You're in luck. I do happen to know a thing or two."

"Oh, really?" Ethan asked, his dark brows lifting in hope.

"Really." She rubbed her hands together. "I just need the proper ingredients, so let's see what we can find."

"By all means, then. Put me to work."

"I'd really rather not use the Bauers' electricity by turning on the industrial-size ovens, and I'm anxious to get back to the clinic and see how the puppies are doing, but I think I know just the thing to make back at the clinic." Now it was her turn to ask. "Do you trust me?"

He grinned, giving her a full view of his perfect white teeth between chestnut-colored lips that looked good enough to bite.

"I do."

"Okay, then. If you can grab a sack of sugar and one of flour from those shelves—" she pointed behind him "—I'll see if I can't manage to scare up some cocoa powder."

He clapped his hands together and headed toward

the rows of neatly organized baking supplies. "I don't know what you're up to, Miss Leavy, but if it includes cocoa, I'm in."

There were lots of things she'd like to do with him that included various forms of chocolate, but she supposed she'd have to settle with baking. Especially since, she reminded herself, no matter how sexy he was and no matter how many unwanted but delicious images he brought to mind every time he graced her with that smile, she wasn't looking for a relationship. Her stay in Singlesville was meant to be permanent.

Having given him an assignment, she made her way to the walk-in refrigerator and, shivering at the climate that matched the one she'd just escaped from, grabbed a carton of eggs.

She opened the door and ran smack into Ethan.

The eggs were safe as she had instinctively pulled their carton against her chest to shield the contents from impact, but when he grasped her shoulders and stared into her eyes, she was very, very far from safe.

"I'm so sorry, June. Are you all right?"

His lips were too close to hers, but yes, technically she was okay. She looked away, fighting to slow the sudden surge in her heart rate.

"Yes, I'm fine," she lied, averting her eyes. "What were you doing here, anyway?"

Perhaps he wasn't immune to her, after all. She caught a tiny jump in the muscle of his jaw, and he was definitely breathing more heavily than the situation warranted. And his pulse was tap-tap-tapping against the velvety skin of his throat, almost in time with her own.

"I was just… I came to check on you. I got the flour and sugar like you said, and, well, you were in there for longer than I liked."

Oh, God, she needed to get away from him. Now.

She pulled back and he let his hands drop.

"Great. I just need to get some vegetable oil and we'll be set."

If she just kept busy, the awkward moment would pass and they could both forget about it.

Ethan cleared his throat but didn't have the decency to stop looking at her. If she hadn't been mistaken, for a second there, it seemed like he might have been on the verge of kissing her.

Far worse, she could not guarantee that she wouldn't have stopped him.

She watched as he moistened his lips, reassuring herself that this was reality and he could not, in fact, read her mind. He could see that, in spite of herself, she would have allowed him to press those lips against hers, just to see what it would be like to have that sensual-beyond-words mouth covering her own.

But the moment was gone forever, and that was a good thing.

It was.

She pushed her shoulders back, remembering where she was and what she was doing there.

"Right," he said. "We'd better get back and check on the puppies."

Her head bobbed rapidly up and down.

"I couldn't agree more."

"You're making what in a what now?" Ethan asked when they were back at the clinic.

June rolled her eyes in exasperation.

"Brownies. In a cup. Like I said."

"I'm not following. I have had brownies a time or two and I really do not see how you could successfully make such things in a coffee mug."

"Well, you'll just have to wait and see, then, ye of little faith."

Having traipsed back through the weather carrying zippered bags of flour, sugar and cocoa, the little bit of oil she'd poured into a mason jar, along with the couple of eggs she'd stuffed in her pockets, they were both dying to eat.

While she'd set out the ingredients on the limited counter space of the tiny break room, Ethan had checked on the pups, returning to say that he'd freshened their water, changed out their potty pad and given them a little more food to eat, and they were snuggled back up for additional, much-needed rest.

The poor little ones were doubtless exhausted from the sheer effort of staying warm in below-freezing temperatures, not to mention having fended for themselves for who knew how long. She knew they would need homes soon, but she didn't want to think yet about giving them away. There was no way she could keep a puppy—not with hours like hers at the pizza place—but their little faces made her heart ache.

So much had been lost to her over the past several months that, even though she knew the tiny creatures did not belong to her, the idea of losing them might threaten to push her over some invisible edge of grief.

"All right," she said, winking at her companion and focusing on the task at hand, trying to block those little brown puppy eyes from her mind, "prepare to be awed and amazed."

Ethan smiled at her, looking ridiculously adorable with his elbows on the counter, chin in hands, watching her like an eager little boy.

She pulled their tea mugs from earlier out of the dish drying rack and mixed ingredients into each one. As Ethan stared, intrigued, she then put the mugs into the microwave. Only a minute and a half later, out popped deliciousness.

She presented him with a mug and stood back, ready to watch him take a bite. When he did, he closed his eyes and remained still long enough to worry her.

"Oh. My. God," he said, barely in time to take another mouthful. "This is amazing."

She shrugged and picked up her own serving. "It's not that exciting, but it's the best I can do with limited time and materials."

"You're being too modest, June. I'm not kidding— this is possibly the best brownie I've ever tasted."

She covered her mouth and a laugh escaped as she swallowed a large bite of moist chocolate. "That's just the starvation talking."

It was true. Microwave brownies were no secret—

they had been trending all over the internet for a while—and she was absolutely not the first one to make them. But in a pinch, they'd have to do.

Out of nowhere, something hit her in the gut, and this time, it wasn't hunger.

It was longing, deep and pure.

She couldn't recall the last time she'd baked anything. Not microwave brownies, not her favorite apple caramel pie or any of her secret cookie recipes that were famous among her friends.

It had been…months.

And she missed it. So, so much.

She had a sudden, desperate urge to bake something for Ethan. Something far better than the stupid brownie he was digging into so hard and clearly enjoying, if the periodic moans he emitted between bites were anything to go on.

While it was absolute bliss to see him loving something she'd made for him, it would be a thousand times more satisfying to see him dive into something really special, something that was truly an original creation of her own.

Baking had been her passion, the one constant in her life. Despite working a full-time job, June's mom had always made time for her when she'd had the chance, time they usually spent in the kitchen mixing up delightful things to eat.

June disagreed with the common conception that baking was a science, not an art. On the contrary, she and her mom had thrown caution to the wind when it came to treats; they played with ingredients and measurements to their hearts' content, never afraid to risk disaster for the possibility of unearthing new greatness.

June released a soft sigh. Those were some of her very favorite memories.

She made a mental note to give her mother a call as soon as she got home, and not another of the short Sunday night check-ins they usually shared, but a real, long, catch-up call. And as soon as she had a break from work, she would visit, and they would bake something fun, something new that neither had tried before.

She could use a little adventure in her life, at least of the safe variety.

Closing her eyes, she poked her spoon around in the last bits of gooey chocolate at the bottom of her mug, the best part in her opinion, and took her final bite of the impromptu dessert. When she slid the clean spoon out of her mouth, June found Ethan studying her, his expression a strangely pleasant blend of curiosity and...joy, as though he'd happened across an interesting painting.

"Something on your mind?" he asked, resting his spoon in his own mug and setting it on the counter.

The way he did that—put down the dish to focus all of his attention on her—was simultaneously intoxicating and unsettling. He gazed at her as though what she might say next was the most fascinating thing in the world, before he'd even heard it. She wasn't entirely sure she liked being examined so intently; there was great potential to make a fool of herself in front of someone she was slowly coming to respect and even like.

She decided to be honest, to be brave.

"The truth?"

He nodded affirmation.

"I was just thinking about my mother."

Ethan's features softened. "Ah, mothers. A complicated bunch, aren't they?"

It was alarming, how much she enjoyed the sound of his voice, that singular mix of accents she'd never heard all in one place before and couldn't quite identify. His words were more carefully formed than the looser, more drawn-out cadence of the locals she'd grown up around; they were tighter but also smoother—not better, of course, just different. And his vocabulary, his way of putting sentences together, was more formal than any man she'd ever spoken to before.

Ethan Singh was a rare, increasingly fascinating gem. He was cool and direct, almost hard, at first meeting, but like a fine baklava, she had the sense he would be infinitely more complex inside, lovelier. Hearing the way he'd talked with his parents on the phone—his tone warm and indulgent, the opposite of his annoyed words that didn't fool anyone—she knew already that he cared deeply for his parents and he placed great value on family.

As did she.

It seemed as the evening progressed, she and the doctor had more and more in common.

"It's true," she conceded. "They are complicated, but I can tell you adore yours."

His cheeks shaded to a slightly darker almond.

"Guilty as charged," he answered, raising up his palms.

June giggled. "An admirable quality in a guy."

"I try." He winked at her and took another bite, not at all shy about how much he relished the experience.

You're doing very well, she wanted to say, but didn't.

"Is she the one who taught you to bake?" he asked. "Your mother, I mean."

June moved to wash out her cup so as to have something to do with her hands. She was used to being in perpetual motion, on her feet all day at work, then crashing into her bed at night. It had been a while since she had been in one-on-one company with someone else for this length of time. To tell the truth, she was nervous she'd run out of things to say—not that she'd said much, as it were—and Dr. Singh, highly educated, was way out of her league.

She rinsed the last bubbles of soap from her cup and set it to dry. "Yes. Or…at least at first."

"Ah. Did you then go to culinary or pastry school before you started at the pizza shop?"

She knew the question wasn't judgmental, but the subject of school was a sore spot for her; her features must have registered as much because Ethan looked suddenly worried.

"Did I say something wrong?" he asked.

"No, not at all." She stopped fidgeting and did her best to show him the same courtesy as he had her, by slowing down to really listen. She knew that must not be easy for a man as busy as he must be—the sole doctor in a clinic that served an entire small town full of furry clientele—so she could at least try to do the same.

She raised and then lowered her eyebrows. "I wish I could have gone to pastry school." She heard the dreaminess in her own words. "In Paris or someplace far off and amazing like that."

She didn't know what else to say, so she simply stopped there. She'd wanted so many things, but the money had not been available, and though she'd worked her butt off to ace her high school classes while keeping up with part-time jobs, her grades just hadn't cut it; they were good, but not exceptional. Not enough for scholarships. And her mom's income had been on that fine line that partially determined the future of so many hopeful kids. According to the government, her mom's finances were healthy enough to put a roof over their heads, to feed and clothe the both of them, and they were too high for her to qualify for aid. But, alas, not enough to help her pay for school. She'd tried combining community college with a full-time job for a few months, but the long days and nights of fighting desperately to keep juggling all those plates had gotten to her, and she'd felt like a failure.

Her mom had wanted June's life to be better than her own, and June wanted to make her proud. She'd let them both down.

"So, why didn't you? Go to school like you wanted, I mean?"

"Lots of reasons." The last thing she wanted was to talk openly about education and money with a man like Ethan Singh, who had likely excelled in school and who, she knew from small-town gossip, was blessed with wealthy parents.

"June," he prodded, his eyes as soft and warm as melted caramel. "I'm sorry to have to tell you this, but that is a pathetic excuse for an answer."

"No, it isn't."

"Yes." He laughed softly. "Indeed it is."

She almost asked what difference it made, but she didn't want to know the answer to that question. The only logical solution was to change the subject.

"Why do I have to talk about my education?" Or lack thereof. "I'd be willing to bet that yours was much more interesting."

His eyes bore into hers for several long seconds and she wondered what he was thinking, what picture he was forming of her in his mind.

It's better this way, she thought.

If he didn't know the truth—that despite her heavy and eclectic reading habit, her attempt to give herself the knowledge she hadn't been able to formally obtain, she'd never be as smart as he was.

She would never fit into his world, even if she had reason to.

At one point, she'd had a chance to be as successful, but that had been stolen from her.

She would get it back—oh, yes, she would—but each time her car broke down or she made another rent payment, she gained fresh understanding that it might well take the rest of her life to do so.

Ethan Singh did not want to hear about that. Heck,

she didn't, either. She'd much rather go back to the beginning of the evening when their only subject of discussion was a pair of precious fur babies.

"Really?" he asked, skepticism written all over his face. "You seriously want to hear about my time at a boys' boarding school and then my grueling years as an intern in the biology department of a university that spent the bulk of students' tuition hiring new football coaches?" He moved his face closer to hers. "I think not."

"Oh, come on. You've lived all over the world, while I've been digging my heels in good ol' Peach Leaf, Texas." She injected an exaggeratedly thick drawl into her words. "So, tell this country girl what it's like in them big, fancy cities."

She was teasing, but when he gave a short laugh in response, it wasn't the full, loose sound it had been before. Was it possible that, in making fun of herself, she'd unintentionally offended him?

How could that be? Wouldn't he have to care for her to be affronted by something she'd meant to be self-deprecating?

"So you really want to know about my past, huh?" Ethan asked.

She nodded, a tad too vigorously.

"All right, then, but this is a two-way street, you know."

"Fair enough," June said, biting her lip. There was something mischievous in his tone.

"So let's make a deal, then, shall we?"

Chapter Six

June forgot everything around her except being there with him, listening to that accent that melted over his words like butter and, of course, sinking deep into those decadent eyes.

It shouldn't have surprised her by then that his charm came with a generous side of cunning. The rules he'd proposed were simple on the surface; she was allowed to ask one question at a time, which he would answer truthfully, but then it was his turn. The problem was, every time he started to speak, follow-up questions popped up in her mind like whack-a-moles, and she was forced to wait until it was her chance to ask another.

It was just that his life had been so starkly different from hers. His father had come to the US to live with

family while attending veterinary college and met his
mother, who'd been working as an intern at the Library
of Congress. Despite their cultural differences—he was
from India and she was American—it was classic love
at first sight. The couple married quickly, and a son,
Harry, and daughter, Sani, had followed before they
finally had Ethan.

Because the senior Dr. Singh had become renowned
in the field of veterinary science, specializing in the
prevention of infectious disease, he was frequently
asked to speak at conferences and even to work on
long-term research projects abroad, always opting to
bring along his family.

"Sounds like a dream childhood," June said, her
voice sounding wistful even to her own ears.

"It was certainly interesting, I'll give you that."
There was a hint of sadness in his tone.

Her eyes narrowed as she studied him. "You didn't
like it?" Such a thing was hard for her to imagine. It
wasn't until adulthood that June had even set foot outside of Peach Leaf. She'd never had reason to complain,
and she knew she was fortunate for the blessings in her
life. But one thing had always bothered her: her world
had always been very small, and she wasn't sure why,
but for some reason that fact made her self-conscious
and overly careful, as though she feared saying something that would reveal a deficit in her intelligence.

He pondered the question for a bit before answering.
"I suppose I did like it sometimes, but like anything
else, it wasn't always perfect."

"What do you mean?" To June, endless opportunity for travel sounded like a dream come true.

"Well, it was lonely, for one thing, moving around so much. Seeing the world was a lovely gift my father gave me and my siblings, but it's not exactly easy to make and keep friends if your address changes frequently."

"That makes sense," she said, not about to remind him that he seemed to have forgotten his own rules and she'd sneakily asked more than one question in a row.

"I suppose there are two sides to every coin." She paused. "I guess I am lucky in that I've always lived in the same place, so I'd have to really make an effort to get away from my friends," she said, chuckling. "Small-town life has its ups and downs. You can't exactly run away from your mistakes, and if you try to forget them, someone else will inevitably be there to fill in the gaps, whether you want them to or not. It's almost like the whole town has a collective memory. Everybody knows everything about everybody else, including all the bad stuff."

He watched her carefully. "You don't seem like someone who would have any bad stuff you'd like to forget, June."

How wrong he was there.

"In fact, you're one of the most thoughtful people I've ever had the pleasure of meeting."

His words came out slow and with intention, as though he'd been planning them for some time, a thought that made her knees a little weak.

She swallowed, careful not to meet his eyes. "You can't possibly know that about me. We've only just met."

"You have a point," he said, "but I don't know many people who would have driven to this office in such a terrible storm to try to save a couple of puppies. Not to mention your reluctance to take food from the Bauers, even though it was compensated fairly."

He was grinning, only teasing her; nevertheless, her cheeks went suddenly warm.

"In fact, I don't need to see much more to believe that the world would be a much better place if there were more like you in it, Miss Leavy."

The next few seconds seemed like an eternity, as the absolute last thing she'd ever expected to happen, happened.

Ethan leaned forward and kissed her—the softest brush of his lips against hers. It was so sudden and so surreal, and over so quickly, she couldn't swear it had even actually occurred. That is, until she opened her eyes and found his face still very near her own, the pleasing scents of sandalwood and lemon blended with something male and uniquely Ethan, tickling her nose. She couldn't keep her eyes from those lips as the corners kicked up in a sultry smile.

Finally, he pulled them away. This was a good thing because June was pretty sure that if he'd left them lingering much longer, achingly close to hers, she would have wrapped her hands around his neck and devoured that mouth, and possibly anything else she could get her hands on.

It had been such an innocent kiss in its softness, yet somehow it had sparked a flame that had rapidly caused her to burn for more.

"You've cheated me, June."

"Hmm?" Apparently he'd rendered her unable to form words, much less full sentences.

"I said you cheated."

"What do you mean?"

"And there you've done it again. Asking questions of me without letting me have a go."

Ah, so he *had* noticed. Evidently she wasn't as sneaky as she'd assumed.

"All right, then. Go ahead." Great, now her voice was embarrassingly creaky.

Way to keep it cool around the hot guy, June.

If she kept this up, he'd regret having kissed her at all, a thought she couldn't bear because now she wanted more, more, more of him.

She glanced up into dark, soulful eyes.

"Here's my question, then. What is it that you'd like to forget?"

"Way to keep it light, Dr. Singh," she joked, but he wasn't having it.

"You know the rules," he said.

She licked her lips, the chocolaty taste of his kiss still lingering there; it took a concentrated effort to refrain from touching them, just to see if the buzz she felt would spark against her fingers.

She focused on the question, organizing her response carefully. Since Clayton had left with everything she had, June had not talked to anyone about how painful that experience was, how badly it had broken her. Her friends pressed from time to time, but she knew her role among them. She was the positive one, the upbeat girl. Letting herself be vulnerable might change how they saw her, and she worried it might scare them away.

She wasn't the one who let her tears show, who wore her heart on her sleeve. She was the one who'd always been the romantic—who'd truly believed that love was out there in some form for everyone, and they just had to find it. She couldn't let anyone see how wrong she'd been, how naive.

"Come on, June. What is it?"

She hesitated. Why did he want to know? And what about that kiss?

Part of her wanted to force the subject, to make him talk about why he'd done it, but the other part was content to just let it be. It would go down in her history as one of the best kisses of her life, possibly *the* best, as it had been completely unexpected, sweet and without any strings attached.

Couldn't she just leave it at that?

No, she could not, and she knew the reason as well as she knew, from an evening of charting them like stars, the pattern of gold flecks in Ethan's brown eyes.

"All right, then. Fair enough." She glanced up at him again, as much to make sure he wasn't something she'd dreamed up as to see if he really did want to know.

"It's a really short story," she started. "There was

a guy. I loved him. I gave him everything I had and planned to spend the rest of my life with him. He broke my heart. The end." She waved a hand, emphasizing the relationship's finality.

Ethan's eyes narrowed and appeared to be full of pain, which was impossible. They were not friends; they certainly weren't lovers. So why did he look so sad? Further, why did he appear as if he knew exactly how she felt?

"I'm very sorry to hear that, June. I truly am. And trust me when I say I've been there myself."

Somehow, she didn't find that the least bit comforting.

"You have?"

"I have. Same song, as they say, different tune."

"Why would anyone...?" She stopped, placing a hand over her mouth. She'd been so caught up in the moment, so enraptured by the feel of those eyes on her, that she'd almost said too much. Her bruised heart needed protection, not more exposure to potential harm, so it was good she hadn't blurted out her confusion over how any woman in her right mind could possibly ruin a chance to be with a guy who, she was quickly learning, was kindhearted, gentle, attentive and thoughtful.

And whose kisses came straight from a fantasy.

"Why would anyone what?" There was a tinge of hopefulness in his expression that she could not have explained for the life of her. So when she heard a low, buzzing sound that startled them both and interrupted their conversation, she almost shouted with relief.

"That's me," she said. "I'd better get it."

Pushing away from the counter where they'd been standing so long her legs were a little wobbly with use, she began following the sound. Finally, she reached her purse, discarded earlier in the reception area, and grabbed it on the last ring.

"Hello?"

"Oh, June, thank goodness." Margaret sounded relieved to hear her voice. "I was worried when you didn't pick up. It's getting late and I hated to call, but I've got some news."

"It's okay. I'm glad to hear from you. It's a long story, but I found some puppies behind the restaurant and ended up bringing them to the veterinary clinic. I've been stuck here with Dr. Singh's son—" she gave Ethan a little wave as he joined her "—for the past few hours. Looks like I might have to spend the night."

"Do you mean Ethan? I haven't seen that boy in years, but last time he was home from college I ran into him at the market. Lord, he's a handsome one."

"That's the one," June blurted. "I mean, not handsome, just that, you know, you've got the right person."

Margaret gave a low whistle. "Sweetie, you are one lucky girl. I'm telling you if I was still young, stuck overnight with a good-looking man like that, I'd make the most of it."

"Margaret!"

"Oh, hush, Junie," she said, but when she spoke

again, her words had softened. "You've been hung up far too long on that damn jerk that broke your heart. It's time you moved on, so if this guy is single…is he single?"

"Yes," she reluctantly admitted, knowing the mess she'd walked into.

"Good, then take my advice—get back on the horse, kid."

June refrained from pointing out the fact that, being in her late twenties, she was hardly a kid, but she knew all the same that her well-meaning boss had her best interest at heart.

"What was it you wanted to tell me?"

"Oh, yes. Hank called a few minutes ago," she said, referring to an elderly restaurant regular that lived in the neighborhood, across the street from Peach Leaf Pizza. "He told me that the power lines are out. Several people nearby have called the electric company and it looks like it could take several days to a week to get things up and running again."

"A week?" June's hand went to her forehead as a series of figures flashed across her mind's eye. A week of no work meant…it meant she likely would not be able to pay her rent the next month without cutting into the miniscule amount of savings she'd managed to scrape together after Clayton had wiped her out.

"That's right." The older woman's voice sagged. "I'm so sorry, honey, but listen, we'll work something out. I did some math before I called you and I'd like to pay you three-quarters of what you'd make if you worked the week. I know it's not the same, and you know I'd give you all of it if I could manage, but without the business coming in…"

"Margaret, stop. It's okay. That's more than generous, but I'll manage."

"Nonsense, June. I…"

"I mean it. I can't take money from you without earning it. I'll be fine."

"I don't like this at all, dear."

"Well, neither do I, but I'm not changing my mind."

Her boss made a dissatisfied noise. "You're allowed to change your mind, hon. Anytime. You know I consider you like my own daughter and it won't do you any good to be proud among family, you hear?"

"I know," June said, emotion welling up in her throat at her boss's kindness. She desperately needed the money, so much so that with an ounce more prodding, any pride she had left would fly out the window. But she wasn't about to take payment without working for it. "But this is final."

"Well, I know stubborn when I see it, and you're a gal after my own heart, but don't you forget that I'm here if you need me. And I want to hear more about those puppies when we're back at the shop. And more about you-know-who, of course."

"All right, that's it. I'm hanging up."

"Details. I mean it."

"Talk to you later, boss," June said, forcing back laughter. "Call me when I can come back to work."

"Hint taken."

"And, Margaret?"

"Yeah, sweetie?"

"Are you going to be okay? With all of this going on, I mean."

"I'll manage. I've got Vince's little Social Security check every month for when the pizza business is slow. Besides, I'm as hardheaded as you are and I've been around a hell of a lot longer, so don't you worry about me."

When she hung up and tucked the phone back into her purse, Ethan's hypnotic gaze was on her again. Her cheeks warmed, remembering that kiss.

"Everything okay?" he asked.

"It has to be." She sighed as the long hours caught up with her, knotting something awful in her shoulders. She'd been going full-force all evening and into the night—first with the puppy emergency, then braving the crazy weather to get something to eat, and finally enduring the shock of that world-rocking kiss. Intense longing for a hot shower and her lonely, albeit warm, bed was almost enough to send her into tears.

"It doesn't sound okay," he said, coming to her side. "And you look tense enough to crack in two." He stood behind her and placed his hands on her shoulders, the touch of them shooting electric warmth all the way down her arms. "Mind if I help?"

Did she mind? Did the man even have to ask?

"No, um, that sounds nice actually."

When he began to rub her muscles, she had to

bite her tongue to avoid moaning. Evidently, his skill wasn't limited to healing members of the animal kingdom; he had expert hands when it came to humans, too. She closed her eyes as the knots loosened and her bones turned to jelly.

Maybe Margaret had a point. Maybe she should take advantage of her limited time with this sexy, tender, animal-loving wonder-god she'd accidentally stumbled upon. With his hands on her like that, did it really matter that he looked like he'd walked off the set of a magazine shoot, whereas her hair had probably frizzed into a puffball and she hadn't set foot in a gym since college?

She didn't like the answer. *Yes*, it did matter.

In case she'd forgotten, the last guy who had wooed her with a fit physique and slick words had broken her heart. She didn't want to be that girl—no, she refused to be that girl—who slipped right into one bad relationship after another.

Ethan Singh might be handsome, and he might even be kind and all the other things she'd seen that night. None of that mattered. She simply wasn't ready to start over, to risk putting all of herself into someone new, only to have it blow up in her face.

Even if he proved to be a good guy, even if he was interested in her, she needed things only she could give herself: time, self-respect and space in which to put her life back together.

Grabbing his hands, she removed them from her shoulders and let them drop as she pulled away and turned to face him.

"Thank you. That was…wonderful, but I—" she hated that hurt expression on his face she'd caused "—I just need a minute. Excuse me."

With that, she left him standing there as she walked quickly away from emotions that threatened to undo her.

Ethan followed, still confused about what had happened.

He hadn't meant to be so forward. Hell, in the space of half an hour he'd not only kissed the woman, but had pulled the most cliché move ever known to man by offering to rub her shoulders.

Dammit, could he be any more of an ass?

What had come over him?

All he knew for sure was that when he saw June hang up from what had obviously been a difficult conversation with exhaustion practically crumpling her body, he'd have done anything he could to make her feel better.

He stopped abruptly in the hallway.

His instinct had been to go after her, to fix the awkwardness that hung in the room after she'd gone, but she had asked for a moment alone. And as his head began to clear, sifting through that spontaneous, intoxicating kiss from earlier, and the way his hands felt digging into her muscles, he realized he needed to give her what she'd asked for.

He needed to back off.

But that kiss.

It made him want to do anything but.

That kiss had wrecked everything he'd been so certain about. Up until it happened, his lips moving toward hers, propelled by a will of their own, he'd been so sure he didn't want a woman in his life. Not when he'd come to Peach Leaf for the sole purpose of getting over the last one.

But with June…it was like he wasn't even in control. Every minute he spent with her made him want another to follow.

Which was ridiculous, considering she'd told him her own heart had been broken recently. What kind of guy forced himself on a woman who clearly didn't want that kind of attention?

What he needed was some air, and for the storm to be over so that he could get her out of his space and off his mind.

When he stepped out the front door, the wind was still blowing with greater than normal force, but it had calmed down significantly since he and June had returned from the bakery. It was a pleasant break from the heat that had developed back in the office between the two of them.

He hadn't expected to feel that way again for a very long time, if not ever. It disturbed him, how much this sensation, this primal drive to be with a woman, resembled those first few days with Jessica.

The two women didn't abide comparison. Jessica had been cool, cosmopolitan, gorgeous in a cold, almost untouchable way, like a model from the cover of a magazine, and fiercely competitive—things he'd admired at first, until he'd discovered the heartlessness she was capable of.

June, on the other hand, was girl-next-door-beautiful, soft and curvy in all the right places and sweet. Sweetness was an underrated quality in a woman, he now believed.

A gust of wind swiped at his face and he had to go back inside. The storm had subsided, but it clearly was not over yet.

Being in the cold made him briefly miss Colorado, and he wondered what June would think of the place he called home, the place he'd lived the longest now and where he'd begun to put down roots. She'd said she had always wanted to travel, and before he stopped the train of thought, it crossed his mind that he might like to take her there one day. Her eyes had sparkled when she talked about wanting to see the world, and that would be a good place to start.

He imagined her face lighting up when she saw the Rocky Mountains for the first time—how drastically more majestic they were in real life than in photos. He would take her to Estes Park to visit the haunted Stanley Hotel, and to Aspen to ski, and the list went on and on, nearly bursting out of him.

Unlike Jessica, who had been near-impossible to impress no matter how hard he tried, somehow he knew June would relish every minute of it, and he longed to feel that way again about a place he loved so much.

As it were, returning would be painful. Those ugly memories would be waiting for him at the university, and even in his home, and he didn't want to face them alone.

"Ethan?"

June had stuck her head out the door to call after him. He turned to follow her inside.

She looked at him like he'd lost his mind.

"What the hell, Ethan?" She gasped, hugging herself against the cold. "You're not wearing a coat." She slammed the door behind them. "What were you thinking?"

He didn't answer the question, ignoring the concern etched in the crease of her forehead. "I'm fine. Just got a little too warm."

The response in her features told him she knew how he felt, but it passed quickly and she forged ahead.

"Ethan, something's wrong with one of the puppies."

His heart lurched into his throat. He'd promised her he wouldn't let harm come to them.

Without speaking further, she grabbed his hand and led him to the back room. When he saw both puppies still inside their little pen, each of them wiggly and energetic, his breathing slowed a little.

"I think one of them threw up," June said, her voice catching in a way that made him ache. "But I can't tell which one."

He crouched down onto his knees and lifted one puppy at a time, palpating their stomachs and checking the rest of their warm, squirmy bodies. When he realized that the pups were completely okay, he almost laughed, but caught himself.

June would be hurt if she thought he was making fun of her for worrying. It wasn't overreacting for her, he reminded himself, because she wasn't used to looking for symptoms like he was. She just followed her heart, an admirable quality.

He put the puppy he'd been holding back into the pen and spent the next several minutes cleaning up and replacing their soiled towels with fresh, warm ones. Then he set his hands on June's shoulders, urging her to meet his eyes. When she did, he noticed glistening at the corners.

"Hey," he said, giving her shoulders a little squeeze. "Hey, it's okay. They're fine." As soon as he'd said the words, a tear slipped down her cheek and, without thinking at all, he reached up to wipe it away before pulling her shaking body against his chest.

He let her cry for a few moments, hating it but wanting to give her a chance to release some of her pent-up emotions. When she pulled back, she wiped her eyes and leaned back on her heels, looking embarrassed.

"I'm so sorry, Ethan. I have no idea what's gotten into me."

He shook his head. "Please do not apologize to me when you didn't do anything wrong."

She grinned, her eyes shimmering with dampness, greener than any emerald he'd ever seen.

"You must think I'm a complete idiot," she said with an unsteady voice.

"Absolutely not. Look, it's been a crazy, long day, and I think we both might be on the verge of simultaneous nervous breakdowns, but don't you ever say you're sorry for being concerned about something you care for."

As she finished wiping her face once more, her eyebrows rose in surprise. "Thank you for that. That's incredibly sweet of you." She was quiet for a moment, and he wondered what was running through her mind.

"I just saw the…" She pointed at the place where one of the little ones had regurgitated its supper, clearly a tad bit grossed out. "And I just lost it. I don't really know why." She tossed up her hands.

"It's okay, June. I'll run some tests again in the morning, but from what I can tell now, they are still holding up really well. It would probably be safest to put them in a crate for the night, but I'd rather not, and this pen is fine."

She nodded and he tucked a strand of auburn hair behind her ear, taking his time in letting his finger slide along her soft cheek before pulling it back. "My educated guess is that they just ate a little too much. Sadly, if they've been without food for a while, it might take some time for their stomachs to get back to normal so they can eat the portions they'll need to gain weight."

June looked as relieved as he felt.

"In the meantime, they'll just need for us to be patient."

He met her eyes as a surge of emotion threatened to overwhelm him.

"After all, this will take some time. What they've suffered simply cannot be healed in one night."

Chapter Seven

The rich scent of coffee brewing pulled June from the short nap she'd finally managed to sink into. Her eyes slowly opening, she glanced around at the unfamiliar room, realizing, as the fuzzy edges of sleep slipped away, that she was in Dr. Singh's office.

The black leather couch squeaked as she pushed up to lean against its back. Chilly, she decided not to give up the blanket that Ethan must have draped over her as she'd snoozed. As the smell of delicious caffeine beckoned her further into wakefulness, her mind drifted back to the night before—and that kiss—the oh-so-delicious kiss that had seared her lips and sent sparks zipping through her veins.

That kiss—spontaneous, incredible, though highly unexpected—made her feel like a woman again.

It was the first time she'd been that close to anyone since Clayton and, she thought with more sadness than she wanted to admit, probably the last.

After she'd had that slightly humiliating breakdown over one of the puppies' mild tummy ache, which she'd replayed over and over until deciding to chalk up her emotions to lack of sleep or an adequate meal, Ethan had dried her tears and sent her to bed, promising to take care of the dogs while she got some rest.

There hadn't been the slightest hint of judgment in his tone or expression, but what had been there instead scared her a little.

She'd looked up into those intense, mahogany eyes of his and found only concern.

He'd been sweet, nurturing even, and had shown her a softness she wasn't used to in men, but she got the feeling that wasn't really Ethan's usual style.

Perhaps the strange magic of a Texas night covered in snow had affected them both. She'd resisted him at first, had not wanted to like him so easily, so much; she hadn't wanted to enjoy his company, but her attempts to not care had been futile, and now her heart had jumped into the game, forcing her to admit that she didn't want their time together to be over.

That sentiment had even kept her from sleep for a while, as she'd tried desperately not to let her eyelids slam shut. But they'd been so heavy from exhaustion, Ethan's voice so soothing as he'd sat in his father's desk chair telling her stories of his Alaskan research trips.

Like a desperate Cinderella, she hadn't wanted it to end.

But in real life, pumpkins weren't carriages and tattered shoes weren't glass slippers…and Prince Charming did not exist.

She needed the reminder; Ethan could have fooled her last night.

But finally she'd succumbed to rest, and it was over. For better or worse, her normal life would resume.

She stretched her arms behind her head before taking a moment to rub a charley horse out of her neck. Wrapping the blanket around her shoulders, she made a quick trip to the bathroom, careful to avoid the mirror, adamantly not wanting to know what she'd be met with following a full shift and a night without a shower. She splashed water on her face and headed to the front of the clinic to check the weather.

"Morning, June," Ethan said, turning as she entered the room. Dark stubble covered his jaw and chin and, instead of looking like hell, which would be perfectly appropriate after being awake for over twenty-four hours, he was even sexier than he'd been the day and night before. And when he graced her with a sleepy smile, she almost threw herself across the room and kissed him. It took effort to remind herself that she'd only stumbled into this situation through a weird turn of events—it didn't truly belong to her. He had not chosen to spend the night with her; it was forced, and he'd been kind to let her stay, as she knew he would have anyone else.

"How'd you sleep?" he asked. "Considering, I mean. I know my father's office couch isn't exactly like a king-size bed in a five-star hotel."

Beds, hotels, unkempt but perfect Ethan with a shadowy beard following a night of…

June shook her head. That wasn't real. The reality was that she'd stumbled upon him due to a freak snowstorm. Reality was, that if the snow had melted enough and the roads were moderately safe, she'd be back at her car and home to her empty apartment in a matter of a couple of hours at best.

The fantasy would be over.

As it should be.

Clayton, with his smooth talking, his well-toned body and those promises he'd made with a straight face while looking right into her eyes—it had all been a fantasy, too. And June needed no reminders of how that turned out.

She may not be highly educated like Ethan, but she was smart enough not to make the same mistake twice. A woman who couldn't trust herself, who couldn't protect her own heart from destruction, was better off alone.

Ethan was staring at her, waiting for her to respond.

"The couch was fine." She smiled. "I can't thank you enough for letting me get a little rest."

He waved a hand, brushing her gratitude aside. "It's nothing. Not my first twenty-four-hour shift, and probably not my last. You get used to it after a few times."

"All the same."

"Don't mention it." He beckoned her to join him at the window. "Looks like we're in luck. I watched the weather on the news a little bit ago and it seems the snow is starting to melt. Also, half the town lost power last night and some won't get it back for a few days. We were pretty fortunate here, with the heater running and all. Would have been a cold night otherwise."

Not if they'd snuggled together, she mused.

He took a sip from the mug in his hand. "The pups were doing great when I checked in and fed them a few minutes ago, and in an hour or so, we'll be able to head out and check on your car."

The news should have been welcome, but for some reason her heart sank. She plastered a smile on her face and crossed her fingers it was convincing. She didn't think she could bear any more of Ethan's insightful kindness or another second of those dark eyes boring into hers, seemingly capable of unearthing her most private thoughts.

"That's excellent news. I can't wait to get back to my place and take a shower."

"I'm with you there. I probably smell like my furry clients," he said, laughing as he turned back to the window.

Outside was a veritable winter wonderland. Snow had blanketed the parking lot, glittering like sugar in the sunlight.

"It's beautiful, isn't it?" he asked.

"Very."

"Have you ever seen snow like this before, June?"

She nibbled her lower lip, stopping, suddenly self-conscious when his eyes followed. "I've seen snow, yes, but never like this. It usually melts so quickly that it doesn't cover anything."

"So you've never really gotten to enjoy it, then? Never built a snowman? Gone sledding?"

She shook her head. His eyes lit up when he'd spoken, and he made all those activities sound so fun.

He tsked. "Well, that is a shame. We get plenty of snow in Colorado, and of course we did during my time in Alaska, too. Most people don't like the weather in the more remote areas, but for some reason, I took to it during my research there."

"Do you miss it?" she asked, instantly regretting the question when a muscle in his jaw jumped, betraying some reaction he probably hadn't meant to reveal.

"I miss the place, not the memories." He was far away somewhere for a moment, but then quickly returned to ask if she'd like a cup of coffee.

"How selfish of me, standing here drinking mine without checking if you want one of your own." He turned, surprising her by tucking a finger under her chin, lifting it to look into her face. "It's been a long time since there's been anyone to ask. Too long."

She licked her lips and his eyes snapped to her tongue. In a matter of seconds, he moved as if to kiss her again and alarms went off inside her, louder even than the one at Bauer's had been.

June pulled her face away from his with effort, disappointment spreading through her body like a virus. If she thought she could let him kiss her again without strings, without involuntarily building an attachment that she knew would be one-sided, she would have allowed it. But that was the thing about mistakes; if you were smart, you learned from them. She supposed she could thank Clayton for that— she knew herself better now, knew she couldn't go in halfway.

It was all or nothing from then on, and nothing was by far the safer route.

Safer, maybe, but a hell of a lot less fun, a little voice chided in her mind.

Unmistakable hurt clouded his features the second she made that decision, but he quickly, expertly erased it.

"I'd love a cup," she said, the air thick with static between them. "It smells amazing."

He nodded, giving her a soft grin. "Stay here. I'll be right back with it."

Ethan was halfway to the break room before he realized he hadn't even asked how June took her coffee. The oversight was just another testament to the trouble he'd gotten into.

She was intoxicating, mesmerizing like a siren, and like a fool, he couldn't stay away from her song.

And if he didn't watch out, he'd be back in the same place, drowning once again as he had with Jessica.

Even though everything in him wanted to do the exact opposite, he would have to be more careful.

He pressed his fingers into his tired eyes, then pulled a clean mug from the dish dryer, a reminder of the night before. Those delicious brownies and those even more delicious lips. The taste of her was almost gone, and he'd stupidly attempted to get it back, only to have June turn away from him.

He should be grateful—at least one of them was thinking clearly.

Grabbing the carafe, he poured her a cup of the expensive, delicious brew his father indulged in and shared with everyone at the office, adding a splash of half-and-half from the fridge and just a little sugar, feeling like an idiot for wanting to get it right. He stopped himself from adding a sprinkle of cinnamon. It would just have to do.

And with any luck, he'd have her back in her car and out of his life soon enough.

He gave the coffee a quick stir and headed back down the hallway, taking a deep breath to steady his nerves.

It had just been a long night; that was all. June was a beautiful, sweet girl, and he enjoyed her company, but that didn't mean it had to turn into anything more.

If only someone could tell his stupid-ass heart the same.

June was still standing at the window when he entered the reception area, the blanket he'd draped over her the night before wrapped around her shoulders.

Her red hair draped across the soft white material, and she looked like an angel.

Which gave him an idea. Snow angels, snow-men—June had never experienced a real chance to enjoy this kind of weather.

"Here you are." She turned and reached for the coffee, closing her eyes as she drew in her first long sip.

"Oh, my God, this is *sooo* good. How'd you know how to fix it just the way I like it?"

"Wild guess. Speaking of wild, finish that coffee and put your coat on."

She raised an eyebrow.

"I'm going to give the pups their breakfast and I'll meet you out front in ten minutes." She opened her mouth to ask questions or to argue, but he held up a finger, stopping her.

"Out front. Ten minutes. See you there."

Ethan's pulse raced and his heart felt lighter than it had in months. He didn't want to believe that it was June making his body behave that way, so he gave credit to the snow. The problem with that theory was that he'd seen a hundred snowfalls, most of them even more magical than this one. Paris, London, New York—the small-town Texas weather couldn't even begin to compare. He loved the idea of sharing this one with someone he barely knew but who'd reminded him that life could go on after heartbreak. He knew there was no future with June for lots of reasons, the most basic being that the two lived in different cities and probably had different goals, but right then, none of that mattered. The only thing he wanted that morning was to show her a great time in his favorite weather.

After checking and feeding the puppies, he threw on his coat and dashed outdoors, regretting that his father didn't keep a sled in his office. The temperature was perfect when he opened the back door and stepped into several feet of powder that reminded him of fresh whipped cream. There was not a hint of the previous day's harsh wind, just cold, crisp air on an occasional whispery breeze. The snow stung his hands as it seeped through his mittens, but Ethan didn't care.

He worked as if in a trance, determined to make June share one of those beautiful smiles with him again, the kind she'd tried to hide after he'd kissed her berry lips. What harm could there be in making a woman smile? It didn't have to mean forever, and it wouldn't. But didn't he deserve a moment's happiness after the way the past year had gone? Didn't June?

Just as he'd thought her name, the woman stepped outside, glancing around before she caught his eye.

"Ethan, what are you up to out here?"

He watched her as she paced nearer, enjoying the way the sun's bright rays danced over her hair, causing it to glisten like a crown adorned with rubies. Her eyes were impossibly green in the dreamlike morning light.

"What's that behind you?" she asked, veering right so she could get a glimpse of what he'd hidden.

He couldn't stop himself smiling like a little boy as he stepped out of her way, waving his arms like a magician's assistant.

June's hands flew to cover her mouth, and those emerald eyes lit up, glistening in the sunshine that reflected off the snow.

Then he heard the best music ever as she threw her head back and laughed, before her feet did a little dance. She squealed. "Is that a snowman?"

"Just for you," he answered, taking far too much delight in her reaction to his simple gift, the only thing he could think to give her for making him feel like the frost inside him had begun to melt a little.

"He's perfect." She held out her arms and spun in a little circle before running toward him. Ethan opened his arms just in time to catch her, but lost his footing as she threw her body into his, plunging them both into the snow.

His laughter mingled with hers, and he didn't at all mind the wetness starting to soak into his back. All he knew was her weight on top of him as she raised up on her elbows and stared down into his face, and the curtain of auburn that came down to tickle his cheeks as she bent to kiss him, her mouth warm and eager, pressing hard into his. When their lips parted, he pulled her close into his chest and held her there for a long moment, unwilling to let her go just yet.

Finally, only when he began to freeze and thus worried that June would be vulnerable to the same, he twisted his body to the side and rose, holding out his hands to help her up.

Her smile disappeared as they stood face-to-face, and all he heard was their matched heavy breathing.

"Ethan, I…"

He covered her lips with a finger. "Shh, don't say anything. Just…just enjoy this with me, will you?"

She was right, of course.

"I get where you're coming from," he said, the words pouring out of him before he could measure them to make sure they conveyed what he wanted them to, not necessarily exactly what he was thinking. "But that's just it, June. I don't want to talk about it, at all. I don't want to try to figure out what's going on between us."

Her eyes had narrowed and there was a crease between her brows.

"Wouldn't you rather just let this be what it is?"

She looked down at her hands.

"That's my point, though, Ethan. We just met. I don't know what this is, and I don't think you do, either."

He rubbed a soggy mitten over his forehead. "I know, I know. But why do we need to understand it at all? Why can't we just enjoy it while it lasts?"

Her expression changed, and as she took time to think of what to say next, he thought he saw something new register.

"I'm not sure where this is going, but I think I see what you're saying."

He waited.

"And, well, the more I think about it, and even though it sounds crazy, you might be on to something."

He took her hand.

"All I mean is that, we both know this thing won't last—it can't, anyway—because I'm leaving in a few weeks and you've got a life here."

She cringed at that last part, but he didn't want to stop and examine that. He needed to convince her to let him spend more time with her, before it was all over. He wanted to soak up her sweetness, to let it seep under his skin so he could take it with him. It didn't need to mean anything more. Maybe not everything happened for a reason. Weren't some things in life just pleasant coincidences?

"We seem to get along, you and I, and if I'm not mistaken, we both had some fun last night, despite the evening not going the way either of us had planned. So while I'm here, and while you've got those puppies for the next few days and they'll need some medical care, let's just enjoy each other."

She bit her lip again, that sexy little gesture that let him know she was considering it.

"But, Ethan, is that wise? You've had your heart broken recently, as have I, and we both need time to mend. Does it really make sense to start something up right now?"

"That's just it, though. We wouldn't be starting anything. Look at it like this. We'll just be having a little fun before we both go our separate ways and get back out there. You're right that we're both unprepared to get into relationships again any time soon, so let's…use each other as practice…for lack of a better term."

He grabbed her hand and pulled her into his

chest, pushing past her resistance. "Let's enjoy each other's company, make each other better and have a few laughs, before we go back to real life. What do you say?"

A look of sadness whispered across her features, but was gone instantly. She smiled up at him, making his heart flutter a little.

"All right, Dr. Singh," she said. "You have yourself a deal."

He placed his hands on each side of her face and brushed her chilly nose with his lips.

He didn't care what kind of fire he might have been walking into, as long as he got to see her again after that morning.

"Deal?" she asked.

"Deal."

With that, he picked her up and swirled her around and around until they were both dizzy, from the spinning, yes, but also probably from something else. When he set her down, June headed over to examine the snowman, giggling with joy over the jerky treat nose, kibble mouth and doggy biscuit eyes he'd scrambled together. As she studied his creation, Ethan knelt to form a snowball, gasping in surprise when one of June's own smacked him right in the middle of his back.

"I don't know why, but it surprises me a little that you like country music so much."

Ethan grinned, the corner of his eye crinkling

behind aviator glasses. Of course they made him look even more stunning.

"Is it because I'm half-Indian?"

She considered his question; she hadn't really thought much about his ethnicity, other than the fact that his father's heritage had obviously given him the most gorgeous, terra-cotta skin she'd ever seen in her life.

"Nope, not that," she said, drawing out her answer to make him sweat a little. He tried to pretend he didn't care, but the longer she spent with him, the more she could see how much he wanted her to like him.

Even though they'd discussed their intention earlier that morning, that whatever their odd little relationship was would not turn into anything serious, it was still a refreshing quality in a man, to be able to see that he wanted to please her.

"I've got it," she said. "I think it's just that country music doesn't mesh with your worldliness or something." She poked his side, making him laugh. "Seems like you'd be more of a classical music type." She eyed him up and down. "I can totally see you fake-conducting an orchestra as you drive to work or something."

"Ah, but that's why I like it so much." He turned and flashed a smile full of perfect white teeth against incredible copper skin. "Reminds me of the simple things in life."

They were in Ethan's large black SUV, headed in the direction where June had left her car. The weather couldn't have been more different than it was the day before; not a cloud in the blue sky, thick mounds of snow gradually beginning to melt as the sun reclaimed her throne. It would take time for the powder to turn back into liquid, and then Peach Leaf would face the possible threat of flooding.

They weren't out of the dark just yet, but things were beginning to look up. She said a silent little prayer that they would find her car in decent shape, but it wouldn't do much good to hold her breath. The old thing wasn't in great health to begin with; it would be a small miracle of it survived the beating it had taken the night before.

Loosening her seat belt a little, June turned toward the backseat to check on the pups. Ethan had nestled blankets into one of the crates from the clinic, then wrapped the little guys inside so they'd be safe on the way to her apartment, where June was thrilled she'd get to watch them until Margaret called her back into work. Ethan had said they'd figure things out from there, but she'd made him promise he wouldn't let anyone adopt them until they were one hundred percent healthy. She wouldn't say it out loud, but the idea of never seeing them again made her stomach churn.

Gently, she poked a finger between the bars, squealing when the male pup bounced over and began to nibble on it. She took that as a sign that he was having a good morning.

That made two of them, she thought, reminiscing about the impromptu snowball fight with Ethan and the adorable snowman he'd built for her, completely out of the blue. She tried not to overanalyze how good it made her feel to be with him, to play, and to have the freedom to kiss him with such abandon without expecting anything serious in return.

She knew it wouldn't last, but maybe he had a point. It was a hell of a lot of fun to be spoiled, to be enjoyed, and even though she hadn't agreed with him at first, she was beginning to come around to his way of thinking. Perhaps their plan would work out fine, after all. No strings, no attachments and, most important, no promises.

Just pure, unbridled fun between two people on the mend. Surely, everything would be fine.

"Okay, that's starting to hurt, mister," she said, taking back her nibbled finger.

"I wouldn't let him do that too much, June. He might start to think it's okay."

"I won't," she promised. "I just like seeing him up and full of energy."

"Well, you'll get plenty of it over the next few days." He tossed a glance her way before refocusing his attention on the road. "Are you sure you want to do this?"

"What? Take care of a few puppies? How hard can it be?"

He coughed out a laugh. "I'd love to hear you say that again in a few days."

She started to retort, but paused as Ethan slowed the SUV.

"Is that it?" he asked. "Your car."

She turned back to the front and caught sight of the old hunk of metal out the front window, barely recognizable underneath a mountain of snow. "Yep, has to be."

He turned off the road, getting as close to her vehicle as he could manage without pummeling into a bank of powder. When the SUV stopped, June reached into her purse and pulled out her keys. Without lifting her head, she grabbed at the door handle only to find Ethan had gotten out, come around and opened the door for her. Such a gentleman. She accepted his offered hand and stepped out of the warm vehicle, which he'd left running to keep the puppies from getting too cold.

By the time they reached her car, moisture had soaked the bottoms of her jeans, but that problem took a backseat to a bigger one pretty darn fast.

She shouldn't have been surprised, but that didn't make it any less annoying when she stuck the key in the ignition, only to find the engine wouldn't turn over after a dozen tries.

Someone in control, someone who had her life together, would have bought a new battery before the weather turned so cold and sapped the last dredges of energy from the nearly four-year-old one. But June had not been so responsible. Between her full work schedule and not wanting to part with the hundred or so bucks a new one would cost, this was what she deserved.

She looked up to find Ethan staring at her, his long body blocking out the sun as he leaned over her driver's side door.

"Thought you were getting rid of me that fast, did you?"

She tossed her shoulders back and tilted her head, debating whether to punch him in those toned abs or straight on the nose.

"What the hell do you look so happy about?" Her question was genuine; shouldn't he be getting tired of her just about now? Shouldn't he be dying to get back to his parents' house so he could get cleaned up and take a much-needed nap?

"Nothing," he said, but the grin didn't fade. He offered her his hand. "Come on, then. No use beating a dead horse."

"I've never liked that expression," she said.

"Neither have I actually, but it suits the situation. There's no point in trying that key again."

She did just that as he rolled his eyes, then shook his outstretched hand.

They tried jumping her car a few times, but it wouldn't take the juice. The old thing had simply given up.

"Come on. Let's get you home. Once you've had something to eat and we get the puppies settled in, we'll call a tow truck."

She hated to admit it, but she liked the sound of that *we*. Exhausted, hungry and craving a near-boiling bath, it was nice to have someone with her, someone who still managed to drum up energy after the long night, someone who put her needs first. It was a good quality in a man...a good quality in a boyfriend...or even a husband.

She almost gasped when the word entered her

mind, but the more she tried to shoo it away, the stickier it got.

Once they got back at her apartment, Ethan was relentlessly sweet, making oatmeal for them both while June took the puppies out of their crate and onto her small back patio. She cheered them on and gave them treats when they went to the bathroom on the least snowy patch of grass she could find, which seemed to come naturally to them since they'd likely been living outside. Her heart ached at the thought of their mother, and she promised then and there that she would take good care of them until she found them good homes. She knew it might not be possible, but she hoped she could find a way to keep them together.

When she went back inside, Ethan had made himself at home in her kitchen, and she couldn't help but think he looked good there. They ate together and he sent her off to take a hot shower while he fed the puppies some of the kibble he'd packed up for her from the clinic's supply closet and texted his vet techs to find out if either of them would be able to drive in and take over that morning while he went home to take a nap.

By the time she finished relishing the steamy water as it thawed her cold skin and wrapped herself in comfy sweats and socks, Ethan had fallen asleep on the couch. The puppies had done the same, snuggled together, safe inside their shared crate with full bellies.

She stood in the doorway for a long time, just enjoying the view. The stunning, kindhearted doctor passed out on her couch after a night spent caring for the two most adorable little fur balls she'd ever seen, all nestled into her small living room.

If she'd been certain it wouldn't wake them all, she would have dug out her phone and taken a photo.

It was an image she didn't want to forget as long as she lived. Instead, she went with her very next impulse. For once, she allowed herself to do exactly what she wanted, without thinking.

Ethan sighed as she lay down next to him on the couch, eyes remaining closed as he drew her against his chest and tucked an arm around her. She looked up just in time to see him smile before drifting back to sleep.

Chapter Eight

"Over here!" June called when she caught sight of her mother's strawberry-blond head passing through the front door a few days later. The coffeehouse, which had the unique luxury of being the only such place in their small town, did not belong to any competitive chains and was especially crowded.

"My goodness," Abigail Leavy said, joining June at the long counter by the window. She set her purse on the bar stool June had saved for her. "Looks like folks got a little case of cabin fever in the storm."

"I think you're absolutely right," June said, standing to give her mother a big hug. "Hi, Mom. I'm glad to see you're okay."

"Hi, sweetheart," the older woman answered, squeezing June in response.

Her mom was tiny and resembled a pixie with her short, stylish haircut, sparkling blue eyes and cheeks that always looked as though they'd been recently pinched. At sixty-five, Abigail looked a decade younger. Despite having worked since she was fourteen, June's mother had not slowed down after retiring from the grocery store, where, over the years, she'd climbed from bagger to manager; the woman made a point of spending time regularly with her numerous friends, walked several miles per day and took pride in her commitment to a healthy diet. June always teased her that she put her daughter to shame.

"Let me go get a cup of joe and I'll be right back." She pulled out her wallet and pointed a finger at June. "Don't you run off now, girl. I haven't seen you in ages and it's getting harder and harder to track you down."

June waved her away and took a sip of her peppermint hot chocolate, a foray from her usual Americano. For some reason, since that first cup of coffee Ethan Singh had made for her a few days ago, nothing she prepared for herself or purchased tasted anywhere near as good.

She smiled, whipped cream tickling her nose as she let her mind circle around and around that man.

Though, at the time, she'd thought that night with him would go down as the longest of her life, it had been nothing compared to the past few days.

He'd gone back to his regular shifts at the clinic, of course, and she'd been happily soaking up her lazy days at home as the power company worked to restore electricity at the pizza place. Only the challenge of training the puppies occupied her time, and she was loving every minute of it.

Despite being busy with the clinic, Ethan called every day on his lunch break to check on her and see how the little ones were doing, and they'd met for coffee once.

But *dammit*, she missed him.

And nothing she tried could make that fact go away. He'd gotten under her skin.

"All right, sweetheart," her mother said, setting a ginormous cup of black coffee on the counter. "Let me just get some of this stuff into my veins and I'm all yours."

"It's certainly no mystery where I got my coffee addiction," June said, giggling.

Abigail took a long sip before putting down her extra large cup. "Come on, girl. You ain't foolin' nobody." She gave June's frothy beverage the stink eye. "That is not coffee."

June looked down into her delicious but admittedly oversweet drink. "You've got me there."

"What's up with that, anyway? Why aren't you having your normal Americano with cream and sugar? What's on your mind?"

"Nothing's on my mind, Mom. I just wanted to try something different."

Her mother glared at her, without a word, and that's all it took for June to break.

"Okay," she said. "Maybe there is a little something on my mind."

Abigail looked a little too satisfied.

"But that's not why I'm here. I really just wanted to spend a little time with you while I've got a few precious days off work."

"That's more like it. I knew something was up. You're usually so chipper, and today you look like you've got a bug in your biscuit."

June snorted at her mom's goofy expression, one of many in the woman's vast collection of odd colloquialisms. Even after hearing it all her life, that particular one still made her laugh.

"It's just the puppies, Mom. Nothing more."

Her mom smiled. "How are those little squirts? Have you given them names yet?"

"No, not yet. I want to, but Ethan—Dr. Singh—keeps discouraging it for some reason."

Abigail was silent for far too long before speaking again. "Ah, so that's what this is about."

June kept her features as neutral as possible, determined not to give in. If her mom caught a glimpse inside her head and managed to figure out how stupidly smitten June was with the doctor, she would never let it go.

She cleared her throat and glanced out the window with as much nonchalance as she could muster.

"That's what *what* is about?" she asked awkwardly. "I have no idea what you mean."

The statement rang false even to her own ears.

Her mom set aside the massive coffee and June knew she was in for it.

"It's this Dr. Singh, isn't it? You've got a thing for him?"

"Mother, I do not…"

"Don't give me that." She held up a palm. "I know my daughter, and I know when she's been bitten by the love monster."

June chuckled in spite of her good intentions. "Mom, you're so silly sometimes."

"Don't you try to change the subject on me. You've got a thing for this guy and I want details."

"Mom," she said, injecting seriousness into her tone as she tried to conjure up sad images to keep from grinning like an idiot at the mere mention of the man's name. "It's nothing. Really, it's not."

"Like you'd tell me if it was." Her words were teasing on the surface, but underneath June detected the hint of hurt feelings.

"Mom." June rested a hand over her mother's and squeezed. "Why would you say that?"

Abigail shrugged. "I didn't mean it, sweetheart. Really, I didn't." Her eyes settled on something out the window, but June could see they weren't focused and her mother's mind was far away.

"I guess what I mean is that, well, I don't see you much anymore."

"I'm sorry, Mom." June cringed. "I had no idea you were feeling neglected lately."

"It's okay. I know you can't help it and I did not mean to guilt-trip you."

"No, really, I'll make more of an effort to see you." June's shoulders sagged. "It's just that I work so much, and when I'm not at the pizza parlor, I'm resting up to *be* at the pizza parlor."

Her mother nodded. "I understand what you mean, June Bug. It was like that for me after your father left."

Her mom didn't talk about her father much, and June had never met the man; all she knew were bits and pieces she'd picked up over the years. He and her mother had never had a real relationship and June had essentially been, as her mom put it, "a happy accident," but she'd always felt loved. Not once had her mom ever made her feel unwanted.

"I've probably never said this before, Mom, but I know how hard you worked to give me the things I needed growing up, and I've always been thankful for it."

Abigail's eyes filled with moisture. "Oh, honey, I did it because I loved you, and I wanted you to have the best I could give you, but all the same, that means a great deal to me."

June's mom wrapped her in a big hug, then pulled her torso back to study her daughter, a hand on each of June's arms. "I just don't want you to make the same mistakes I did."

"What do you mean?" She sipped her lukewarm hot chocolate.

Abigail released her and then did the same with her own drink. "Well, you work so hard, and you've always been so independent, like I was. I certainly

can't blame you for that, because you got it from me."
She winked a pretty blue eye. "At the same time, I
don't want to see you miss out on the same things
I did, honey."

"What mistakes, Mom?" she asked. "When I look
at you, all I see is a strong woman who worked hard
her whole life, who has a daughter and lots of friends
who love her."

"Oh, sweetheart, thank you."

"I mean it—I don't see any mistakes."

Abigail's forehead creased as she studied her fresh
manicure.

"Surely there were times when you were a kid that
you wished your father was around or that I didn't
work so much."

June nodded. "That's true. I did wish those things
sometimes, but if my father didn't make you happy,
and if you wouldn't have been happy with him in our
lives, then I trust that you made the right decision."

"He wasn't a bad guy, but he didn't want to be a
dad, and no kid needs that kind of burden. Plus—"
she gently touched June's cheek with her palm "—I
was so excited to have you, and you were such a
sweet little thing, always smiling and happy to see
everybody."

Though there had been times when she'd wished
for a brother or sister, it was true that she'd enjoyed
a happy childhood, and she knew that some kids
didn't have any parents; she was always just glad to
have one that loved her so dearly.

"I'd love to see you back to your old sunny self,

Junie. I know you're working hard and you probably won't let me, stubborn girl, but is there anything I can do to help?"

June shook her head. "I'll be fine, Mom. Just need to keep working and save up again so I can change things." She swallowed, wishing she could believe it would be that simple to start over. "I'll find a way."

"I know you will, sweetheart." Abigail paused. "I swear, if I could find that Clayton Miller, I'd kick his ass into next year."

June laughed so hard she almost snorted hot chocolate out of her nose. "I know you would, Mom. I know you would."

"Seriously, though, don't work yourself too hard and forget to live your life. You're too young for that." Abigail's voice quieted, her tone softening. "I dated a guy once, back when you were little—a good one— and I should have let him in more. He wanted to build a life with us, and he was so wonderful with you, which mattered to me more than anything else, but for some reason—I guess because I was too afraid to let any man near us again because he might disappoint you like your father did—I let a very good person go. Now I can't tell if that was the right or wrong choice, and life's too damn short to dwell on such things. But I'm telling you this because, if it happens to you, I don't want you to miss out on love by being afraid that what happened with Clayton might happen again."

June's eyes were tearing up, and she dabbed at them discreetly with a napkin, not wanting to attract attention.

"The point is, I don't want you to stop living life to the fullest. No one can promise that your heart won't get broken again, but if something good comes along, don't be afraid to take it, June Bug."

"Mom, I can't…"

"Just promise me you won't be too scared to try flying again."

She pulled in a breath, then released it slowly. "I promise."

"June?" Her ears picked up the low, smooth voice in the distance and she turned.

"Ethan. Hi," she said, standing up from the stool, righting her cup after nearly tipping it over. *Very smooth indeed.*

He waved over the crowd, so tall she had no trouble seeing him. His hair was still damp from a shower and he'd shaved all that sexy stubble off, which would be a pity if he didn't still paint a gorgeous picture. He wore a deep silver button-down shirt the color of storm clouds, the sleeves rolled up, revealing toned forearms with a coating of dark, silky hair.

The thundering in her heart increased as he neared, women looking up from their tables to catch a glimpse of him as he passed. The thing that really set off her pulse, though, was that he didn't notice a single one of them; he had eyes only for her. She wondered if it was possible that he'd gotten more handsome since she'd last seen him a few days ago.

When he stood only a foot or so away, the intoxicating scent of his skin caused all rational thought to fly out the window.

"June, it's so great to see you here," he said, seemingly unsure of what to do with his arms. For a man who had previously exuded confidence, seeing him a little flustered was just plain cute.

Her little heart completely ignored her and went to town—the traitor.

"It's good to see you, too," she said, helplessly grinning from ear to ear. "The puppies are doing really well. My neighbor—who is supertrustworthy, by the way, and has a rescue dog of her own—practically jumped at the chance to spend a couple of hours with them."

"That's wonderful to hear," he said, reaching out to touch her forearm, a gesture that was both unexpected and incredibly intimate. His touch tingled all the way up her arm, making the fine hairs stand at attention.

Good Lord, the things he could do to her with such simple, innocent contact.

She wondered if he had any idea what kind of effect his presence had on her. On her body, her mind, deep inside her most intimate places.

"But how are you doing?" he asked, lowering his head to make up for their difference in height so he could stare straight into her eyes. Heat blossomed in her belly and spread all over.

"Me? Oh, I'm... I'm good," she stammered. "Thanks for asking."

"Ahem." The sound of June's mom clearing her throat startled her and Ethan.

"Ethan," she said, turning to include her mom,

"this is my mother, Abigail Leavy. Mom, this is Ethan Singh, the veterinarian I told you about."

His eyebrows rose in response to that last part. "Ms. Leavy," he said, and June reminded herself to thank him later for not assuming she was a *Mrs.* "It's so very nice to meet you."

"Likewise," Abigail said, flashing those baby blues at him. "I hear you were quite the hero the other night, saving those puppies."

June was tickled to see his cheeks darken. Suave, classy, worldly Ethan Singh, blushing over a simple compliment? She hadn't thought she'd live to see the day and, of course, she made a quick mental note to tease him relentlessly about it later.

"I was just doing my job. It was nothing out of the ordinary."

June's mother practically burst out, "Oh, I'm sure June would disagree."

"Mom," she said through clenched teeth. "I'm sure Dr. Singh has to get back to work."

"It's true," he said, those illegally sexy lips curving upward. "But I was hoping I could borrow you for a moment first, June. There's something I'd like to talk to you about, if you can spare the time."

"Oh, she absolutely can. Can't you, sweetheart?"

"Yes, Mother." She turned and shot daggers at her mom. "I think I can take it from here."

"I certainly hope so. Remember earlier when I advised you ought to say yes to a good thing, should one come along? Well, this is exactly what I was talking about, so do yourself a favor," she whispered quickly to June, then turned and offered Ethan a million-dollar smile. "I'll leave you two alone," she said. "Call me later, June Bug."

Abigail picked up her purse and remaining coffee and hurried off, blowing her daughter a kiss over her red acrylic fingernails.

June rolled her eyes, but was unable to help grinning at her mother's tenacity.

Ethan watched the older woman go, then turned to June. "She's a firecracker, that one, isn't she?"

June chuckled. "That's one way of putting it."

"She seems like a lot of fun."

"Never a dull moment with Mom around." They both stopped talking, and uncomfortable silence filled the space between them until he motioned for her to sit down. He took her mother's chair.

"There's something I wanted to ask you, June."

She nodded, then took a sip of her now-cold drink and immediately regretted it.

"A friend of mine, Isaac Meyer, owns a companion animal training facility in town."

"Oh, yeah," June chimed in. "Friends with Fur."

"Oh, so you know it. Good."

"Well, not really. I mean, I've met Isaac and his wife, Avery, but I haven't ever been to their facility, though I have heard only good things about it."

"Yes, it's excellent. Isaac and Avery are really great with animals and they do a lot of important work in the community to encourage people to rescue shelter pets. Anyway, what I wanted to ask you is, they're having an event next Sunday that I thought you might like to take the puppies to."

"The puppies?"

"Yes, well, it's an adoption event, where people can come and see rescue animals and get to know them a little—see if they want to apply to take one home."

Her heart lurched into her throat at the thought of giving away either of the dogs she'd grown so fond of after the past few days. She swallowed, reminding herself that the animals did not belong to her; soon, they would need permanent homes, and it would be her duty and responsibility to help them find forever families.

Besides, there wasn't room in her life for a pet right now, much less a brother and sister pair.

So why, then, did it hurt so much to even think about letting them go? Especially when that's what was best for them.

Ethan continued speaking, and she didn't think he'd noticed her hesitation. Thank goodness for that at least; she had no desire to explain something she couldn't even understand herself.

"I think it would be a great way for them to have a chance to find homes, don't you?"

"Yes," she agreed, her voice a little squeaky. "Of course I do."

"Good, so you'll come with me, then?"

"Sounds like a plan."

"Oh, and that's not all," he said. "What time should I pick you up tomorrow?"

"Tomorrow? What's tomorrow?"

"Don't tell me you've forgotten."

All she could do was stand there, mouth gaping open.

He crossed his arms, grinning. "You really don't remember, do you?"

She absolutely *had* forgotten.

"My niece, Neena's, birthday party. Remember, when we were at Bauer's Bakery and my parents insisted I bring you by and you seemed okay with it."

"Oh, my gosh! I can't believe I forgot. Ethan, I'm so sorry."

Mixed emotions surged through her at the thought of spending time with him around his family, at how intimate that would be considering they'd agreed that this…thing…would not get serious.

Not serious, sure. And here she was about to get introduced to the people who cared the most about him.

"My family can't wait to meet you, and after all, you did promise you'd go."

She must have looked as nervous as she felt because he gently squeezed her forearm, chuckling. "Hey, they don't bite. We don't have to stay long, but you'd be doing me a major favor. If I don't bring you, I'll never hear the end of it."

She swallowed down the nervous lump that was taking up far too much space in her throat. "I did promise, didn't I?"

He nodded, clearly enjoying the sight of her squirming far too much.

"All right, then. It's just meeting your parents."
The words nearly choked her. "It'll be fine. What's
the worst that can happen?"

Chapter Nine

The following Sunday, June found herself victim to the oldest curse known to woman. There she stood in front of a closet full of clothes, yet she had absolutely nothing to wear.

"I really need to give some of this stuff away, huh?" she muttered to a furry audience of two. The puppies were curled up on a towel in the cushy dog bed Ethan had given her to take home from the clinic, and when she spoke, their little heads tilted adorably.

She didn't know too much about dogs, having only ever had a cat, but she could tell that the puppies were starting to learn a few words after only a couple of days. After observing that, she'd started intentionally naming things when they were exposed to them, like their water, food and toys.

At first, trying to keep track of them had been challenging—she'd started a little notebook to record their eating and potty schedules so she could take them outside at regular intervals and to avoid accidents. Ethan taught her that it was better to try to keep those from happening altogether and instead to give the puppies treats when she took them outside and they were successful.

If someone had told her a month ago that she'd be that interested in the bathroom habits of a couple of baby border collies, she would have questioned that person's sanity.

She laughed.

Yet here she was recording everything the little ones did. Beyond enjoying their company and going through their daily routines, she hadn't thought much about the mechanics of caring for them, but it occurred to her suddenly that she'd basically become a dog mom.

And, oh, she loved it so much.

Being an only child and then working so hard all of her adult life, June had never really given much thought to having kids, but every time she cleaned up a little mess or woke up in the middle of the night to take the puppies outside, she felt a little less afraid of the idea of having a child of her own someday.

The thought of children reminded her of Ethan, whose family was large and full of kids.

Oh, gosh. Ethan!

June's eyes flew to the clock on her nightstand and then absorbed the chaotic hurricane of clothing scattered all over her bedroom. Skirts hung from the closet doorknob; tops littered an armchair in the corner; there were bras and underwear hanging from the lampshade and the unused elliptical trainer. Still, she hadn't settled on anything yet, and he was due to pick her up in less than five minutes.

The doorbell rang, sending shock waves up her spine.

Oh, God.

Her hair was still wet and she stood there wearing nothing but a towel.

That was another lesson the dogs had taught her—they always needed more time for bathroom breaks than she planned for. If they weren't so cute, she'd be tempted each time she took them out to shout at them to pick a patch of grass already—they were all the same, for goodness' sake.

But they took their time, and now she had none left.

So she did the only thing she could think of, digging through the fashion debris until she found her pale blue bathrobe with the fluffy white clouds on it. She could only hope that when Ethan saw her wearing it, he wouldn't instantly change his mind about taking her to spend time with his family.

"Coming," she called out as he pressed the doorbell one more time.

She moved as quickly as she could, wanting to curl up and die when she opened it and saw Ethan standing there, the perfect specimen of modern masculinity. Beneath his unbuttoned overcoat he wore a navy-blue, long-sleeved henley and dark jeans. His hair waved a little above his collar—she loved that it was just a little too long—and his face was clean-shaven.

There wasn't even a trace of the annoyance she'd thought she might meet when he saw that she wasn't anywhere near ready to go. Instead, his toasted-almond eyes twinkled as he looked her up and down, making no attempt to hide his approval.

Wait. Was that really what she'd seen in his expression? The perfectly put-together, insanely gorgeous Dr. Singh had just seen her at her most unkempt—wild, soggy hair that hadn't had a proper trim in months, old, ratty bathrobe that she'd thought whimsical when she'd purchased it and which now just seemed childish and not a stitch of makeup.

After looking down at herself only to confirm that, yep, it was as bad as she thought, she finally worked up the courage to meet his eyes.

"Ethan, I'm so sorry I'm running late." She wrung her hands and flicked a thumb in the direction of her bedroom by way of explanation. "The puppies…"

He crossed his arms over his wide chest—firm, too, she knew, after the closeness they'd shared the other night.

"Not what I'd expected, but I see nothing to complain about." He winked at her. "My parents and siblings, on the other hand, well, they might not be so keen on…"

"Ha, ha," she teased, opening the door wider so he could come in.

As soon as he did, two little black-and-white fuzz balls galloped over, their ears bouncing up and down.

"Well, look who it is," he said, crouching down to scoop them up.

She was tickled to see that he didn't care at all about his clothes getting hairy. That quality made her like him all the more.

"Have they been behaving for you?" he asked, moving farther inside the living room and sitting cross-legged on the floor.

June closed the door and sat on the couch, extra careful to wrap the robe tightly around her body. The way Ethan had eyed her in the doorway made her think about things she probably shouldn't. Being pretty much bare underneath the robe increased those feelings until they hovered at a dangerous level and she had to force herself to think of anything but... that. Anything but being naked and alone with a man who made her insides burn with need.

She focused on the question he'd asked.

"They've been great," she said. "I've gotten their feeding schedule down pat, and potty training them has been a cinch, thanks to your helpful tips."

"Are they eager to get treats for following through with what you ask?"

Good, she thought. If he kept the conversation along that line, she'd have no trouble forgetting her growing fantasies about what it would be like to...

"Yes, they seem to want to do what I ask as long as they know they're getting doggy snacks. Is that a good thing?"

"Definitely. It means they're food-motivated, so

as long as you're handing out the goods, they'll aim to do what you need them to."

"I've had my neighbor, Ainsley, and her dog, Max, over to work with them, as well. She's the one I was telling you about who sometimes fosters dogs, and she'll be watching the puppies tonight as soon as I text her to come on over."

"That's great, too."

"What is?"

"That they're spending time around an unfamiliar human and dog. That will help get them socialized so that when they're ready they can go to good homes even if there's already a dog living there."

Her heart lurched and she started to ask him when he thought that day might come—she wasn't even close to being ready for it—but she closed her mouth, quietly watching for a few moments as he rubbed their tiny bellies. "I'll leave you here with them and go finish getting ready."

She headed to the bathroom and closed the door, resting her back against it as she tried to slow her breathing.

Every time they were apart for a few days, and then she saw him again, things got so much worse, meaning, she wanted him so much more. The sparks between them had become more frequent and much stronger and she could feel the chance of an explosion increasing at a terrifying rate.

Since running into each other at the coffee shop, he'd called each day, often more than once, and he'd even stopped by a time or two for a few minutes to ensure that the puppies were thriving.

Each time they spoke on the phone, and when he'd come over, she could sense that he was going through the same thing—wanting to take some elusive next step with her, but afraid of what that might set in motion.

The other morning when they'd had that snowball fight, and after briefly discussing what to do with their casual, not-friendship, not-relationship thing, it had all seemed so risk-free.

Surely, if they had agreed not to let things get too emotionally serious, then they were both on the same page and that very thing would not be allowed to happen.

But then, what about all the physical longing? What about the way her body seemed drawn to his by some unseen force? What in the world were they supposed to do about that?

If they let things get too far, she couldn't be certain that she would be able to inhibit herself from wanting some kind of commitment, something more permanent. She could not promise herself that she would be able to indulge in getting physically closer to him without her heart following along.

Neither could her growing affection for him be ignored.

But she didn't think she could stand to be in the same room with him for much longer without giving in to temptation.

And that's exactly what she faced that day—hours

and hours by his side without being able to touch him the way she wanted to, tell him what she was going through every time he was around.

It would be absolute torture, she thought as she pulled on a pair of dark purple skinny trousers and a soft, silky black sweater with sparkly gems along the collar. They were the first pieces she'd put on earlier and then discarded in the bathroom, and now, with a tornado of garments covering her bedroom floor, it was of course what she ended up wearing. It was an outward testament to how little she trusted herself these days.

Her favorite outfit, the only one guaranteed to act as a confidence-builder, and along with a pair of black high-heeled boots, it would have to do.

Because Lord knew, she needed confidence that day more than ever before.

A soft knock rapped on the other side of the door and she opened it.

"I'm sorry to bother you and I don't want you to feel like you have to rush, but I just got the puppies to sit on command, and I wondered where you keep your treats."

"Oh. Of course." She passed by him into the hall-way, catching that light but heady scent that hung on his clothes and skin, and started to head down the hall toward the kitchen; but Ethan caught her hand and spun her to face him.

He pulled her to his chest until her forehead touched his chin, then put a palm on either side of her face and covered her mouth with his own.

Shots of electricity buzzed up her spine as the moist heat of his tongue touched hers, deepening the kiss. Without thinking, she wrapped her hands around his hips, tucking her fingers just under the hem of his shirt, moaning when her skin made contact with the warmth of his.

Encouraged, he moved his hands to her shoulders and backed her up until she was against the wall, both of them gasping for air as they gave in to the heat between them.

Finally, she pulled away from his mouth, forcing breath into her lungs.

"What was that for?" she asked, a smile playing at the corners of her lips.

As she fought for composure, Ethan just stood back and flashed that sexy grin of his. Though his motions were smoother than hers, she could see the way his chest rose and fell rapidly, and her own swelled with pride that she'd agitated him to such a degree.

"I just wanted you to know," he breathed, "how beautiful you look today, June."

She coughed out a very unsexy laugh. "Thank you. Very much. But my hair's still wet and I haven't even gotten around to putting on makeup yet."

He stepped closer, threatening to start it up all over again. She wanted to cross her arms over her chest, to keep him at a distance, but her body wouldn't let her. It seemed to crave his in a way she couldn't control.

His eyes plunged into hers. "I meant what I said," he whispered, leaning in again.

She worried he might kiss her once more. Somehow she knew that if he did, there would be no chance of them making it to the party.

Instead, he brushed his lips against hers in the softest of touches, then let her go, padding back down the hall, leaving her breathless and shaken to her very core.

Half an hour later, standing outside an entirely different door, Ethan possessed even less control than he had when he'd arrived to pick up June.

He'd anticipated that evening all day.

Yes, he wanted to see his family, especially his niece Neena, whose tenth birthday they would be celebrating, but the bulk of his eagerness he'd have to attribute to seeing June. He'd been looking forward to a casual, fun evening and maybe an equally casual kiss at the end of it, but when she'd answered her door wearing that tattered old robe, her red hair wet and in complete disarray, she had absolutely thrown him for a loop, caught him totally off guard.

It wasn't hard to imagine her naked under that robe, and after pressing his body up against her in the hallway of her apartment, he could trace her curves in his mind's eye with no effort at all.

She was even more beautiful that way than she'd been when they first met the other night. Without any adornment, her green eyes shone clear and bright, and her hair was like satin as he'd weaved his fingers through it. She had a body that was made to be adored—ample curves for a man to hold on to, soft, creamy skin…it was such a shame he would never have the chance to be that man.

The way she'd responded to him back there, the way she'd reached under his shirt to dig her cool fingers into his burning skin and kissed him back with abandon, he knew he could have her. He knew it wouldn't take much to get her into his bed.

So why wasn't he doing just that?

He watched her face out of the corner of his eye as they stood outside his parents' front door, his heart going soft at her nervous expression.

"No worries, June. My family is a mess but they are nothing if not kindhearted. They will love you, trust me." He squeezed her hand and didn't let go.

Something knotted in his throat as he said the L-word. The last time he'd used it had been for Jessica, and he'd expected using it now to leave a bad taste in his mouth.

But it didn't. And what he'd said was perfectly true. His family would love June, which distressed him to no end.

The only time he'd brought Jessica to meet them had been awkward and uncomfortable for everyone. She simply didn't fit in, did not understand his family's warm teasing, the way they'd tried to get her to open up to them and to make her laugh. She'd been like oil to their water, everything they said hitting her the wrong way and prickling under her skin.

It was a day he'd like to forget.

It didn't escape his understanding that he was bringing Jessica's polar opposite with him this time, fully aware that she would be met with a completely different reaction.

They would love June's sweetness, her easy smile, her softhearted nature and her sense of humor.

All the things *he* loved about her.

That thought crashed into him like a sucker punch, and he thanked his lucky stars when the door opened and his mother wrapped him in a bear hug.

"Ethan, sweetheart, I'm so glad to see you," she said far too loudly into his ear.

"No need to shout, Mother. I'm right here," he said, grinning.

Melanie Singh whacked him in the side and turned her attention to the woman next to him.

"And you must be June," his mom said, folding her hands together in front of her. He knew that meant she was trying not to be too huggy and it made him cringe. Jessica had complained about his family being overly physically affectionate, a trait he'd never noticed until it had been pointed out to him. A trait he happened to treasure.

He'd grown up feeling loved and surrounded by affection. Of course, he'd apologized on their behalf when Jessica had complained, hating himself for doing so when, even at the time, he'd known it was she who'd been too cold.

A smile spread over his lips as he watched June hold out her arm, as if to invite his mother in. The two women embraced like they'd known each other their whole lives, and seeing their instant connection set off butterflies in his stomach.

"I'm so happy to meet you, Mrs. Singh," June said, holding his mother at arm's length, her eyes sparkling as she chattered easily. "Ethan's told me so much about you. I've heard lots of stories about all the places you've visited as a family, and I'd love to hear more from you if you have the time."

"Absolutely. Oh, I'm so glad. I think sometimes we embarrass our boy, and I hope you'll forgive us if we roped you into something you weren't wanting to do, but we're just so proud of him and we're so excited he's met someone new."

His mother gave him a pointed glance that said a thousand things all at once—the topmost being that she instantly liked this girl he'd brought into her home.

And though he did not like what such a thing implied, not in the least, knowing that his mom approved of June pleased him an inordinate amount.

He would have to keep that to himself. If his mother knew, she'd have the two of them married before Neena's party concluded.

"Come inside, you two, and let me get your coats. How silly of me, letting you freeze out here while I yammer away."

June laughed and followed his mom inside, tossing a smile over her shoulder as he closed the door behind them.

Inside his parents' home, after their coats were taken, they were met with a flurry of friendly chaos as siblings and their children, aunts, uncles and anyone else collected along the way descended upon them. June's eyes glowed at the rainbow of saris worn by some of the Indian women in his family. Several others wore jeans and T-shirts, but June's eyes were drawn to the rich jewel-toned fabrics of his father's place of birth.

"They're all so beautiful," she whispered when they had a second without anyone's attention on them. "I feel so plain in my outfit."

"Nonsense. You look amazing." He pulled her close so that his lips touched her ear. "I thought I made that quite clear earlier."

He loved the rosy apples that instantly blossomed in her cheeks at what he'd said. Images flooded his mind of all the other areas her skin might turn pink for him in exchange for whispered words.

She looked at him, her eyes huge under bright fairy lights that were strung all over the house. "I mean it, though. Are you sure I'm dressed okay?"

"Absolutely." He touched her elbow to soothe her. "You would look beautiful in traditional Indian clothing. Don't get me wrong. But no one expects you to wear it. I would have told you if that was the case. See," he said, holding a hand out to encompass the room. "Plenty are dressed similarly to you, so you fit in just fine."

"Good," she said. "I was a little worried I'd under-dressed."

"Not at all. Just breathe, June. They already think

you're wonderful—my mother in particular, and that's not a common occurrence."

Me, in particular, he'd really wanted to say.

She looked down at her feet. "I'm so glad."

"Ethan!" He turned from June to see his brother, Harry, hurrying across the room with open arms. Harry grabbed him, then greeted June with his usual, friendly bear hug, making her laugh.

"Is my brother bothering you?" Harry asked, sending June into giggles. If the man wasn't already happily married with two excellent children, Ethan's hackles might have risen. Harry was stupid-handsome and taller by several inches than any of the other Singh men. But he was also too sweet and goofy to invite jealousy. He teased June for several minutes until she was almost doubled over in laughter. Finally, Harry's wife, Amani, caught Ethan's eye, rolled her own and came over to join her husband.

"Take my advice," Amani fake-whispered to June, "and stay far away from this family, unless you want to become crazy like the rest of us."

As she spoke, Amani tossed adoring eyes at Harry and he gave her a big smooch on the cheek. The four of them bantered for half an hour about the couple's recent vacation, how Ethan was managing the clinic, Amani's work in civil rights law and their children, Neena and Suresh.

"Neena's having a blast," Harry said. "But I'm afraid she'll be disappointed when she finds out she's not getting the present she asked for."

Amani's soft eyes met Harry's. "She'll be all right.

I think between the cake, her grandparents and aunts and uncles spoiling her and her friends, she'll forget all about it."

Harry glanced at Ethan and then June. "Neena's been asking for a puppy since she first started to talk. I would love to look in to getting one for her, but Amani insists that she and I are too busy to take care of a pet for Neena. Between you and me, though, I think she's at just the right age to start learning the responsibility of caring for a pet."

Amani gave Harry a worried look, but he brushed off his wife's concerns.

"You worry too much, my love. The best way to teach her responsibility is to give her some. What do you think, Ethan?" Harry asked.

Ethan glanced between the two.

"Ordinarily I'd say not to drag me into it, especially when I know Amani will always win—" he winked at his sister-in-law "—but in this case, I'm inclined to agree with you, Harry."

"Well, that would be a first," his brother teased, gently punching Ethan in the shoulder.

"No, I mean it. I think you might be on to something. There are plenty of studies supporting the idea that children who are given pets to care for at a young age—with their parents' supervision backing them, of course—become more caring, conscientious and reliable adults."

Amani tilted her head. "Truly?"

Ethan nodded.

She put a finger on her chin. "Wow, I had no idea.

I mean, it makes sense, but I didn't know there was evidence to back it up. You might have to send me some of those articles, Ethan." She leaned closer to him and June. "And don't you dare tell my husband this, but if you're right, I might have to consider changing my mind," she said, plenty loud enough for Harry to hear. "Besides, you know I love dogs."

Ethan looked at June to see if she was tracking his line of thought, but her eyes were aimed down at the glass of champagne someone had placed in her hand earlier.

"And it so happens that I may have just the puppy for her."

At that, June's eyes snapped up to his.

Something wasn't right, but he couldn't read her expression. He would ask her as soon as they had a moment alone. It was possible she was just feeling a little overwhelmed; his family could have that effect on new people.

Harry and Amani seemed interested in hearing more, and he had two puppies to find homes for, so he went on. "As a matter of fact, that's part of how June and I got to know each other. It's a long story, but the short of it is that she came into the clinic during the storm the other night and was carrying two puppies with her."

Amani put a hand over her heart and her face softened as he told them about June's rescue, unable to hide his pride in her.

"Anyway, if you'd like, June and I can bring the pups by later this week and Neena can meet them."

As he spoke, Ethan's brother and sister-in-law nodding in agreement, he noticed June's skin had turned a little pale. As Harry and Amani discussed the idea of their daughter getting to see the dogs, he took the opportunity to ask if June was all right.

"Me? Oh, yeah," she said, her voice faltering a little. "I'm fine."

"Are you sure, June?" He placed his hands on her shoulders. "Look, if this is too much, being here with all these people you haven't met before… I mean, it might be too much, just let me know and we'll get out of here."

"No, Ethan, it's not that, it's just…"

"All right," Harry burst in. "We've talked it over and we think it's a great idea. As long as you don't tell Neena what the plan is. I just want you to make sure you don't say anything about her possibly getting to keep one, since my wife isn't completely sold on the idea yet."

Ethan pulled his eyes away from June for just a second.

"Hang on one sec, Harry." He turned back to her, and her features had released some of the tension that had been in her face. "Are you okay, sweetheart?"

"Yeah, um, yes." She closed her eyes and took a deep breath before speaking again. "Yes, I think I will be."

He touched his fingertips to her elbow, willing her to feel his tenderness toward her, to know that her will was his command. "Are you certain you wouldn't like to step outside and get some fresh air?"

June shook her head and he forced himself to let go of the issue, hoping that by now, she would surely tell him if he'd done something to bother her.

It shouldn't matter, he knew.

They were merely friends, destined to end that friendship when they parted ways in a short time.

But something was changing between them, something that made him believe it did indeed matter. The puppies, what she thought of his family, and of course—most of all—how she felt about him.

Warm awareness prickled up his neck.

All of it mattered.

Chapter Ten

The ride home from Neena's party was the epitome of awkwardness, and June kicked herself for being the cause of the uncomfortable silence. Ethan had asked her what was wrong more than once, but had given up the third or fourth time she told him it was nothing.

But how could she tell him what was really bothering her? He would think her silly, or worse, she might scare him off if she opened up her heart that much. What had been bugging her for the week since they'd met, since she'd been the main caretaker of two new little lives, had only become crystal clear to her as of that night when Harry had brought up giving one of the puppies to his daughter and Ethan hadn't objected.

She knew it was nothing personal, knew he wasn't deliberately trying to hurt her by rushing to find homes for the puppies—he was only doing his job and trying to make sure they were cared for—but it made her heart ache nonetheless. She'd finally figured it out, and she wanted to share her thoughts with him, but she wasn't brave enough. If he knew what she'd realized, it would be too much for him, too serious, and he'd run.

Ethan pulled his SUV to a stop outside her apartment and walked her to Ainsley's unit to pick up the puppies. Once they were back inside June's home and had put the dogs to bed, there were no buffers left; she would have to face him.

He took her hand and led her to the couch, his eyes tender as he brushed a piece of hair back from her cheek, rubbing the auburn strand between his fingers before tucking it behind an ear. The way his gaze held hers the whole time made butterflies gather in her stomach, their wings tickling her insides.

"June, look, I know something's been on your mind."

She pulled her eyes away from him and down into her lap, focusing on the sad state of her nails.

"Look at me, June, please," he said, tilting her chin up toward him. "I know that this—" he waved a hand between them and she understood that he referred to their odd pseudo-relationship "—is weird. But the fact is, well, I've begun to care for you." He swallowed, his nervousness out of character. "Quite a lot actually."

Her eyebrows lifted and one corner of his mouth kicked up in response.

"I know. I didn't mean for it to happen, either. It just did." He closed his eyes and sucked in a deep breath, and as he let it out, the impact of what he was trying to tell her pummeled into her.

"We don't have to discuss the way I feel, or if... if you're feeling something similar—" she opened her mouth to speak, but he held up a palm to give her pause "—and, in fact, I'd rather not do it tonight. There's always time for that later."

She closed her lips. They both knew there wasn't going to be time later, not if he left Peach Leaf and they both went their separate ways.

"But as I said, I care for you, June." He reached out and took her hand, flipping it over to rub a finger against her palm.

The touch resonated all the way up her arm and sped up her breathing.

"So I *do* want to know what's been on your mind that you've not been telling me."

June swallowed and took some time to gather her thoughts. She wasn't ready for this, especially after hearing his confession that he'd developed stronger feelings for her than he was supposed to have let happen. If he hadn't stopped her, the chances were high that she would have blurted out the fact that she was going through the very same thing, if not something even more.

She wasn't ready to put a label on it, was most certainly not ready to call it...*love*. But that flutter under her ribs each time she saw him, that gravitational power he seemed to have over her that made her want to get as close to him as possible—none of it could be denied anymore.

Add to that the new knowledge of how sweet he was around his family, how much she'd enjoyed watching him play with his nieces and nephews and the way he supported his brother and sister and welcomed any stranger as a new friend, and the evidence was clear. Maybe it wasn't quite love, not yet at least, but one thing was for sure; she absolutely adored Ethan Singh.

Still, she couldn't tell him the truth just yet—that she'd begun to think of the puppies as a symbol of the new life she was trying to build. That, somehow, even though it didn't entirely make sense, she'd begun to believe that if she failed the animals, she would fail herself. She knew she didn't have the resources or the time to nurture them and be there for them the way she should, but neither was she willing to let them go.

If she gave up on them, she felt, it would be as if she'd given up on herself.

Worse, selfishly, she knew that once the puppies were no longer her responsibility, Ethan would have no real reason to see her anymore.

A week ago, she hadn't known the dogs or Ethan Singh, and now the loss of all three was a real threat, a specter of darkness hanging around her future.

Imagine if she told him all of that; she wouldn't blame him for wanting to disappear from her life. And she wasn't ready to face it herself.

Still, he stared at her, waiting for a response, the question of what was on her mind hanging thick in the air between them.

Maybe it would be safe to tell him just a fraction of the truth, especially since, for whatever reason, it seemed to be almost impossible for her to lie to the man. He acted as her own personal truth serum.

"You said you don't want to talk about this tonight, and, well, I guess I'm feeling some of the same things you are. I think that this thing between us just overwhelmed me a little tonight, meeting your family and all."

"I'm sorry, June." He smoothed a hand across his forehead. "I shouldn't have pushed you into going."

She shook her head. "No, don't apologize. I agreed to go and you didn't push me. It's just that I hadn't imagined how much I would enjoy being around them and I guess the thought of never seeing them again—after you're gone, I mean—is a little sad to me."

His lips formed a thin line and his eyes narrowed as he considered her words.

"Maybe it doesn't have to be like that," he said. "But let's not talk about the future." He leaned in until his lips were mere inches from hers. "Right now, I want to know only one thing."

"Mmm," she mumbled, apparently unable to form whole words when he was that close to her.

He smiled and ran his tongue along his lower lip, moistening it. "What can I do to make you feel better tonight, in this moment?"

"Anything?" she asked.

"Anything."

Instead of spelling it out, she wrapped a hand behind his neck and slowly, tentatively, pulled him in, pressing her lips against his, relishing his signature taste—cinnamon, as always, from the chai he drank so often, layered with a hint of champagne from the party. Emboldened by his hungry response as he wrapped his arms around her waist, she parted his lips with her tongue, deepening the kiss, smiling against his mouth when he gave a soft little groan.

She moved her hands from his neck, over his shoulders and down his muscular arms, grasping his hands in hers. She moved them to her breasts and he responded by softly massaging the mounds over her sweater, her nipples rising to meet his touch.

She groaned in protest when he moved away.

"June," he said on a heavy breath. "Are you sure you want this? I mean, don't get me wrong, I absolutely, definitely do, but I don't want to pressure you. I know we're both just out of bad relationships and I don't want to..."

She held up a finger to quiet him. "Shh. Don't think so much, Ethan. Just go with it."

He smiled, lips parting to reveal perfect teeth, and she grinned in response. "I can do that," he said.

"Good. That's what I hoped you'd say."

He kissed her again and ran his hands down her sides, pausing at the hem of her sweater. When she nodded briefly, he lifted it slightly, tucking his hands under the fabric. His hot fingers against her skin, still cool from being outdoors only moments before, caused a slight intake of breath, and then she relaxed into his touch as his hands slid up her back. They slowly, expertly glided along her spine, then back down, circling around to the front where he smoothed them over her abdomen. When they trailed upward to her chest, his fingers toying with her nipples until they perked up to meet him, she closed her eyes and relished the sensation.

When she opened them again, she met Ethan's dark irises, his pupils dilated with arousal, letting her know he'd like some attention, as well.

So she moved until her back rested against the arm of her couch, pulling him until his torso rested against her. She was glad that a certain part of him was far away from her hands, though she could feel him growing when his groin came in contact with her thigh, the knowledge that she'd turned him on so thoroughly setting off her own response.

She ran her hands up his back, stopping here and there to admire the muscles before running them back down to his abs, and then to the waistband of his jeans. His mouth covered her own as he grabbed her hand and guided it to the front.

June didn't hesitate in removing his belt and unzipping his fly.

But that was as far as she got before her nerves settled in. Ethan seemed to understand that she needed to slow down a bit, and he lifted his upper body away from her, pulling her over until she rested against his chest, his arms wrapped around her. She looked up and saw that dark stubble she loved so much beginning to show along his jawline. He smiled down at her, his eyes full of desire but warm and patient. She rested her face against his chest and attempted to slow her breathing.

Was she really ready for this? Had she truly healed enough from the last person she'd been with, the person who'd so completely shattered her heart, to be able to give herself to someone new?

Even if they'd agreed that this wouldn't turn into a relationship, she still owed Ethan that much, that he would be the only man on her mind without her dwelling on the past if they went through with this; she forced herself to use the actual words—if they made love. She wanted to give him her whole self, not a broken collection of parts. He deserved that, just as she did from him.

When she looked into his eyes again, she found confirmation that she was the only woman on his mind; he wasn't far off somewhere, recalling the last time he'd held someone like that. The way he gazed at her, making her feel like she was the most beautiful, most amazing woman in the world, told her she had all of him.

And, for that night, that's all she wanted. It was enough. It had to be enough.

With renewed confidence, she placed a hand on his shoulder and pulled her body up, straddling his waist with her legs.

"God, you're gorgeous," he said, as breathless as she felt. His arousal was there between them, causing June to long for more from him. She kissed him again and again, until hunger mounted on both sides and they couldn't stand it there any longer.

In one quick motion, Ethan rose from the couch, lifting her as if she weighed nothing.

For once, she was more than satisfied with the size of her apartment, as it was so small and uncomplicated she didn't have to point out where the bedroom was.

Ethan smiled at her as he carried her there, laying her down gently on her lavender bedspread, shoving aside the clothing she'd discarded earlier.

He lifted her legs one at a time to pull off the socks she'd worn inside her boots, stopping to kiss the ticklish parts of the soles of her feet, making her giggle.

She was thankful for his lightening the mood, as intensity had begun to build and she knew they were both close to breaking. He seemed to know instinctively when she needed a softer moment before he started in again, sending desire spiraling through her.

He pulled off her pants and tossed them aside, then she leaned up until her head was at the level of his torso. His jeans were still undone, so she made quick work of removing them completely, her pulse rocketing up as she ran her hands along his firm behind, covered only by black boxer briefs.

She looked up at him and he nodded, his eyes black as night in the dark bedroom. With her eyes locked on to his, she pulled off the underwear, running her hand along his hard length until he shut his eyes and his legs slackened.

"June, I can't survive this much longer," he said, grabbing hold of her hand. "I want you."

She smiled and pulled him down onto the bed, where he relieved her of her own underwear, leaving only her bra and top. His hands worked fast but gently, pulling her sweater over her head and unhooking her very last piece of clothing.

When all of the garments were gone, they stared at each other for several seconds. June loved the contrasting colors of their skin, her lighter tone against his darker one, and she couldn't wait to blend them together into one.

Ethan softly pressed her shoulders back until her head lay on a pillow. His hands slid up her thighs until they reached her center, and he spread her legs, then bent forward to kiss her, plunging his tongue into her mouth as he caressed her heat, slipping a finger inside. When she was very wet, she grabbed a condom from a drawer of her bedside table, allowing him to slip it on before he dove deep inside her.

Everything faded away until all that was left was his pulsing, faster and faster until her core buzzed with desperate need. At his final plunge, they burst open to each other until there was nothing left to give. And when Ethan slid from her body, he lay down behind her, pulling her against his warm form.

Both of them wordless from exhausted pleasure,

he ran his fingers through her hair and along her arm, until she drifted off into the deepest sleep she'd enjoyed in as long as she could remember.

A terrible noise ripped Ethan from sleep, and it took almost a full minute for him to realize where he was, and that the god-awful sound was an alarm tone coming from June's phone on her bedside table.

He almost laughed when he looked down to find her still in his arms, her eyes slammed shut, completely oblivious to the ripping sound.

"June," he said, chuckling. "June, wake up before I throw that damn thing across the room."

One eyelid rose revealing a pretty green iris, but fell again almost immediately and it took several more tries before Ethan was able to fully wake her.

"Good Lord, woman," he said. "You sleep like the dead."

She stretched out her arms and tossed a sleepy smile in his direction. He crossed his arms over his chest and watched her, just enjoying the view. The sun wasn't up yet, but when she flicked on her bedside lamp, soft light flooded over her ivory skin and all that luscious red hair fell over her shoulders, rendering June so ethereal and beautiful that she resembled a wood nymph.

Her beauty was unique and warm, and he wanted to wrap himself in it like a blanket. As fresh thirst began to build, he reached for her, ready to quench it with her body.

But as June picked up her phone, her eyes widened and she launched out of the bed before he could catch her.

"Oh, my God, I am going to be so late for work." She ran to her dresser and grabbed clean underwear, mumbling to herself. "So late, so late, so late!"

Ethan had to get to the clinic himself to relieve the night vet tech, but he wanted to enjoy the show for a few more minutes—June's naked curves moving quickly around the room as she gathered clothing. He didn't know when he would next get the chance to see her like this, and he wasn't about to miss relishing that moment; it would be worth arriving a half hour late to work. It would also be the first time, so he was confident his father's vet tech would forgive him.

He leaned back and rested his torso against the headboard. "June," he said, but she didn't register him calling her. "June!"

This time, she looked up as if from a trance, and her eyes softened as they landed on him.

"Yeah?"

He curved a finger. "Come here for a second."

If he was honest, he enjoyed the battle raging in her eyes, clearly weighing the cost of missing work with another hour of lovemaking with him. It had been the best of his life with June, without contest. For the time being, coming off a night of it, he'd be willing to give up everything to spend another day wrapped up with her in those lavender sheets.

As it were, he would never get her out of his mind, and he could already tell that the day at work would be the longest of his life. Finally, the battle was over, and he was disappointed to realize that she'd made the mature, adult decision.

Dammit.

"I can't, Ethan. I've got to get to work."

But at least she walked over, her berry lips curved upward, and his eyes latched on to her creamy breasts as they hovered above his chest when she leaned in for a kiss.

"I really do have to go," she said, the very same moment he took her forearm and pulled her down on top of him. His heart buzzed at the giggle she gave in response.

"Ethan," she said, trying her best to be serious. "I'm going to be late for work, and it'll be pretty hard to come up with a legit-sounding excuse when Margaret's already given me a full week off."

"But I'm not finished with you yet," he argued, attempting to strengthen his case by nibbling at her neck and dotting tiny kisses along her shoulders. "There are so many spots I haven't yet kissed."

She indulged him a little, but finally pulled away. June put her hands on either side of his face.

"Last night was...amazing. It was beyond amazing," she said, echoing his thoughts, "but it can't last forever." She ran her thumb along his lip, sending vibrations all throughout his body.

"Do you know what you do to me, June?" He grabbed her hands and held them to his chest. "Do you have any idea?"

She closed her eyes as he felt his heart beat against

her fingers. "I have some idea," she answered, eyes wide and full of desire, "if it's half of what you do to me."

He grinned at that and leaned in to kiss her. She kissed him back with the same hunger that tore at his insides. Everything in his body burned to take her again, to be inside her, where he felt better than he ever had before in his life.

It was even possible that he...

"But I really do need to get out of here." She took her hands back from him and touched his face once more before rising from the bed. As she stood before him, hands at her sides, doing nothing to hide her form, he let his eyes wander from her lovely, fiery mane, past her spectacular breasts, all the way down to her purple-painted toes.

"You're the most beautiful woman I've ever laid eyes on, June." He'd thought the words might come out cheesy, and that June might rightfully laugh at him, but his voice was strong and as he spoke them he realized that no truer words had ever escaped his lips.

And then it hit him.

What the hell had he done? What had he allowed himself to get into here?

He hadn't meant for things to go this far. Obviously, he'd wanted her physically more than he ever had anyone else, but he'd sort of convinced himself that, once they'd slept together and the novelty wore off, the mystery was gone, that things would calm down between them.

He'd mistakenly believed that he could get the woman out of his system.

On the contrary, she was more present in him, had more of a grip on him, than he'd thought possible.

Instead of getting her out of his system, he'd invited her in, all the way.

And he knew now that nothing he could do or say would get her out.

He swallowed, bringing a hand to his forehead to brush off the beads of perspiration that had sprung up there.

She was right to get away from him now, and he would let her go.

He dropped his hands to his sides.

"Right," he said. "Right, you should get ready for work and I'll do the same or we'll both be seriously late."

Something in her features let him know she'd registered the sudden change in his demeanor, but she didn't have time to question it.

He offered a small smile, hoping she wouldn't ask about his abrupt decision to come around to her way of thinking.

Thankfully, she turned and left the room.

If she'd stayed, she would have seen the way he buried his face in her pillow for what he somehow knew would be the last time, inhaling her sweet jasmine scent. If she'd stayed, she might have heard him groan as he realized what a mess he'd turned their casual non-relationship into. And worst of all, if she'd stayed, she might have seen the first bud begin to grow as love—yes, *love*—blossomed in a heart he'd thought dead.

Chapter Eleven

On Saturday morning just a week after she and Ethan first made love, June's hands shook as she pulled into the drive at his parents' home. She turned off the ignition and forced herself to take ten deep breaths.

She couldn't put her finger on why she felt so nervous all of a sudden. She and Ethan had been seeing each other off and on the whole week, Ethan taking the puppies to work each day with him and bringing them to June's to spend the night. Just the puppies, though, not Ethan himself.

Maybe that was the problem.

Something had changed after they'd slept together, but it wasn't the type of thing she expected. Sure, now and then a guy spent the night with one of her friends and never called again, and it had happened to June once a long time ago, but this was something entirely different.

Ethan still called, he still visited, and if anything the two had gotten closer...but they just hadn't been to bed together again.

And it was making her insane.

This was exactly why they had agreed to keep things casual, and yet he'd gone and taken it to the next level.

She stopped herself, recalling that perfect night a week before.

Her assessment wasn't fair; she had been the one to take that first step, and she'd been more than happy when he went along with her. Without a doubt, it had been the best night of her life. Ethan had been wonderful—attentive, but not demanding, letting her take the reins, but giving as good as he got—and, oh, he was an amazing lover.

The problem was that he was also more than that. She'd seen a change in him that next morning when she'd been running late for work. He'd been so tender, so...well...*loving*. He'd been in no hurry to leave and had even packed her a lunch while she'd showered, and then had driven her to work and kissed her when he dropped her off, promising to call that afternoon—a promise he then kept.

She knew what the problem was; it was all too good to be true.

At least now she had her own car back, complete

with a big-ass bill for a new battery and the cost of a tow.

She rested her head on the steering wheel for a moment before opening the door and lifting the puppies out of the backseat in their crate, along with a tote full of baking supplies.

She slammed her car door shut with a foot, careful not to jostle the puppies too much, and then she looked up just in time to see Ethan jogging in their direction. Her heart swelled the second she met his gaze, further proof that something wasn't right.

Over the past few days, she'd had plenty of time to realize that she had been kidding herself when she'd agreed to keep this thing with Ethan casual. It would be easy to blame it on the way their physical relationship had changed, but in her heart of hearts, June knew it was so much more.

As she watched him approach, she was reminded once again just how much she genuinely liked this man, how incredibly, purely happy she was in his company. No one had ever made her come alive the way he did, and she had him to thank for bringing her natural optimism back. She'd even gotten the urge to bake again and to risk hoping that she might still someday see her dreams come true.

He was special, no doubt, and he'd gotten a hold of her in a way that no man ever had. Not her horrible ex—not anybody.

She recognized the feeling for what it was, but still she resisted naming it. Doing so would solidify it, somehow, and she wasn't ready to do that just yet.

Because she knew that, the second she did, it would all be lost. If Ethan found out what was going on in her heart and in her mind, he'd back off and possibly out of her life. And she didn't want to, but she needed him now. Though he was still as wonderful as ever with the puppies, it also had nothing to do with them anymore.

"Hey there," he said, drawing up in front of her, reaching for the tote bag and dog carrier. "Let me take those from you."

He leaned forward and kissed her cheek before leading her to the door.

Though they had seen each other since that night they spent together—doing the puppy exchange and going out to dinner a few times—this was the first time they'd be in a house together. She prayed she could keep her hands off him, keep from making a fool of herself by wanting him to sleep with her again when he'd made no motion to take her to bed over the past week.

She got the sense he was being careful with her, as though he didn't want to hurt her. But not being with him again, after they'd shared each other that way, hurt even more.

He led her through the door he'd left propped open and she followed as he brought the crate and bag into the dining room that attached to the Singhs' kitchen. He pulled a few child gates out of a linen closet and set them up. "So we can watch them while we go in the kitchen," he said.

June nodded.

Ethan glanced at a clock on the wall. "We've got about three hours until we have to be at Friends with Fur. Anything you'd like to do until it's time to go?"

June's cheeks went warm at the same time Ethan's turned a slightly darker shade and she knew he'd heard it, too. Of course there were things she'd like to do in that time, all involving clothes on the floor and lots and lots of bare skin.

He cleared his throat and looked away, disappointment clouding his features.

Her heart sank and she changed the subject before the sharp pain could do any more damage.

"I brought baking stuff, and I was thinking we could make some canine treats for the adoption fair if that sounds good to you."

He managed a soft, sad smile, but it was a smile nonetheless, and she would have to take it. "That sounds like a great idea."

He took her hand and led her into the kitchen. He asked what he could do to help and she gave him the task of measuring out the dry ingredients while she whisked together eggs and water in a small bowl.

"This isn't my recipe," she said, leaning against the granite countertop to admire the Singhs' chef-worthy kitchen. "I found it online. But I did make a few modifications that I think will make these biscuits even better."

Ethan glanced over his shoulder. "I'm sure they'll be excellent," he said, his voice sounding distracted. He stirred flour and baking powder together in silence for a bit. Finally, he turned to face her, dropping the wooden spoon to his side.

"Listen, June. I…"

She put the bowl down and held up both palms. "You really don't need to say anything."

"I would like to, though. I feel like we need to talk and we're both dancing around an elephant in the room, hoping it will go away. But, June, it won't. We have to discuss some things."

"Actually, you're completely wrong. That's the beauty of our little arrangement. You said friends only, nothing serious. So we absolutely don't have to talk about it, now do we?"

She noticed, too late, that her voice had gone up an octave, making it all too clear that she was agitated, that she cared far too much. Of course, the way they'd set things up, caring *at all* was too much.

He closed his eyes and then put down the spoon, crossing his arms over that toned chest she'd loved resting her head against. "I know that's what we said, but I don't think either of us can deny that our boundaries really don't apply anymore."

She tilted her head. "Of course they still do, Ethan." Without them, there was too much freedom. Anything could happen between them if there weren't any limits, and she just wasn't ready for that. Was she?

His brows lowered over stormy eyes. "How can you act like nothing happened between us, June? How can you stand here baking dog cookies like nothing's changed at all?"

"I don't know, Ethan. You tell me. It's probably

the same way you can take me out to dinner and then leave for the night without even kissing me goodbye."

He brushed a hand over his face. "You're right. I know I've been doing it, too." He looked up and met her gaze, his eyes burning with the same things she felt but was too afraid to speak out loud. "But don't you think it's time to cut the crap?"

She was quiet for a moment, knowing that anything that came out of her mouth had the potential to define their relationship in permanent ways.

She stood at a precipice, looking down into a pit, the bottom of which she couldn't see and held both danger and possibility. Here was her chance. Here was a guy who was willing, pushing even, to define what was going on between them, and maybe even to acknowledge that they both wanted more.

An amazing, kindhearted, hardworking, absolutely gorgeous human being obviously cared for her. Wasn't that what she'd always wanted? Wasn't that her dream? Hell, wasn't that every woman's dream?

So why would she even consider cutting their conversation short and throwing it all away, which was exactly what she knew would happen if she refused to engage in that discussion with him?

There was too much at stake. Their hearts were both still too tender from being broken by careless people. Not to mention the fact that, even if she wanted him to stay with her, or better, to go with him, she knew she couldn't have that. Could she?

"I think the crap, as you called it, is the only thing saving both of us from making a huge mistake."

The look he gave her then—that look that said all the things she couldn't articulate—nearly undid all of her resolve. It would have, except that she'd succeeded in her goal of getting stronger, of resisting the temptation to give her whole heart to someone again. As much as it hurt, she wasn't going to open her heart and tell him how she really felt. She sure as hell wasn't going to admit to him, or even to herself, that she was falling for him so fast she couldn't keep the walls from caving in on her.

"June," he said softly, unwinding the strings around her heart as he stepped toward her, "I'm not so sure anymore that it would be a mistake."

She closed her eyes so she wouldn't melt into his.

"So, how can *you* be so sure?" he asked.

She gasped when his cell phone began to buzz in his pocket.

"Aren't you going to get that?"

"No, it can wait. We're having a conversation here."

She turned away. "I think you should take the call."

Even though she was no longer facing him, June could feel the heat from his eyes blazing into her back. She felt sick. She'd been rude and awful, and she wanted to kick herself for it.

He didn't deserve this. Ethan was a great guy, willing to rehash their initial boundaries so that they could talk about their growing feelings and possibly go forward. And what was she doing?

Acting like a complete and total immature idiot.

She groaned and turned around, ready to apologize,

but was met with Ethan's broad back. He was stirring the ingredients again and the only indication that anything had changed was the forceful, angry way he beat at them with the spoon. And, of course, the thick, tense ball of terrible energy that had taken up all of the air in the room.

Her nerve endings were frayed so that June felt everything at double the normal intensity. Standing there, watching the moment slip by, with her heart hanging off a cliff, June wasn't sure if she was relieved or furious when his phone started up again.

His head tilted backward against his upper spine and then he looked back down, hands clenched into fists at his sides as if he fought to gather his composure.

He picked up his phone, voice tight as he greeted the caller.

She didn't know who was on the other end, but she was grateful for the chance the call gave her to pull herself together. Now that she'd elected to forego a conversation that could have changed her path, her entire life, all she could feel was a tight disappointment in the pit of her stomach, the absence of anything good.

She knew instantly that she'd made a severe mistake, and it would cost her if she didn't fix it. The problem was, she didn't know how.

Before Clayton, she'd been an open book, a romantic, a heart-on-her sleeve kind of girl, but he had crushed that out of her when he'd stolen her life savings and skipped town without so much as a text or a note. She'd spent the following months trying to figure out what had happened, how her dreams had seemed so clear, right at the tips of her fingers, only to disappear overnight.

It wasn't the only time her life had changed in such a short amount of time. The other night when she'd made love with Ethan, it had changed again, but this time she didn't feel like curling up in a ball and quitting; this time, it had made her want to grow wings and soar.

But she couldn't tell him, because if she did and he didn't return her feelings, didn't want the same new life with her, where would that leave her? She had nothing left anymore; if she let Ethan have her heart and he broke it, all that would remain would be a shell of a person, and June would rather not become someone she would grow to resent.

She stood, unable to get her limbs to move until Ethan finished his call.

When he turned around, all of her raw emotion was reflected in his eyes.

He fidgeted with the phone and then finally slipped it into his pocket. "I have some good news," he said, and she could see that he was trying to offer her a smile.

She put her hands in her pockets, afraid that if she didn't give them something to do, they might reach out for the man she'd begun to fall hard for. So. Hard.

"Yeah?" she asked, but the word came out more like a choking sound.

"Yeah, um…" He raked a hand through his hair "That was Harry, my brother."

"I remember," she said, folding her hands in front

of her torso, hoping he would understand that she meant she remembered far more about that night than the names of his family members.

"Right." His eyes were dark and narrow as he studied her. "Anyway, he says that Amani is on board and they want to take one of the puppies for Neena, after all."

"Oh," she said, not making any attempt to inject joy into her voice. She certainly didn't feel any, and this new revelation only made that worse. But if it would make him happy, she would lie. Just this once, because she needed to see light return to his face. "That's—" she swallowed over the pain rising in her throat "—that's wonderful. I know they'll be the perfect family for one of the puppies."

But what about the perfect family I want?

"I thought so, too. They love and respect animals and they'll take good care of a puppy." His eyes were tired now and his shoulders sunk as if he felt defeated. "We should go," he said, glancing at his watch. "Isaac will be expecting us soon."

Had that much time passed? She checked the wall clock and got her answer. No, it had not. Ethan probably just wanted to get away from the suffocating room, away from her. She didn't blame him—she wanted away from her, too.

Friends with Fur was bustling with activity when Ethan and June arrived less than an hour later. It was early—dog food and supply vendors and animal rescue organizations were still getting their booths and pens set up—but he couldn't have stayed in that kitchen with June for a single minute longer.

Seeing her struggle to talk to him about whatever it was she was feeling, and not being able to communicate himself, had been the worst form of torture. The sadness in her eyes had made him want to run, to get away from her, because what could possibly be causing it, if not his presence in her life?

When she'd come into his clinic a couple of weeks ago, she'd been like a breath of fresh air, her passion for saving those puppies only a fraction of the kindness that defined June Leavy. From that instant on, he'd wanted nothing more than to get to know her better, to get lost in her sweetness so he could forget about Jessica and his broken heart.

He'd told June that the boundaries he'd set, the "rule" that things wouldn't get too serious, were for both their benefits. But in reality, his doing so had been purely selfish. He saw that clearly now—now, when it was probably too late.

He'd tried to protect his own heart from getting broken again, but he truly had not realized that doing so might be the very thing that would cause her pain. It caused him pain, too. Keeping her at a distance had been a mistake. He realized that now. But if she wouldn't talk to him, wouldn't tell him what was wrong, how could he help her?

He hadn't thought it possible that they would end up wanting more from each other, and now that he knew that to be the case, he had no idea what to do about it.

This had not been in his plan. Their short-term relationship was supposed to be casual, a stop on their respective routes to healing from past heartbreak; instead, falling for her and not being able to do anything about it for fear of hurting her was causing more harm than good.

And still, she was sweet to him, letting him hold her hand as they walked around the open training arena inside Isaac's facility, June having insisted on carrying the crate with the puppies inside. They were getting bigger and would need their own separate crates soon.

For some unknown reason, even though he'd been campaigning to find them homes, the thought of giving them away so soon, especially to separate families, caused his throat to catch.

"Ethan!"

He turned to see Isaac Meyer, his wife, Avery, and Avery's dog, Foggy, headed toward the two of them. Isaac shook his hand and he introduced his friends to June. He couldn't help but smile as he watched June ask to pet Foggy, and Avery, who was always just a bit shy, seemed to take to her instantly.

That was his girl—warm, kind, drawing people to her like bees to honey.

"Are these the puppies you've been telling us about?" Avery asked, crouching down to peer into the crate.

June's eyes brightened and her whole demeanor changed as she regaled her new friend with stories from the past couple of weeks. She'd gotten so attached to the little guys.

And suddenly it hit him—he'd been awful about the puppies. Nonstop, he had talked only about finding them homes, giving them away, thinking it was the right thing to do. And all the while, June had been falling in love with them.

That must have been why she had become so distant the past few days, and why her thoughts had gotten so far away each time he mentioned Neena wanting a pet or bringing them to the adoption expo.

By dragging her there that day, he had, against her will, set in motion events that would break her heart yet again. He hadn't been careful with her feelings the way he so badly wanted to be, and he'd overlooked the fact that the puppies really did in fact belong to June. He didn't have the right to make decisions about them without consulting her, and now he wanted to kick himself for neglecting to put her needs first.

"You know," Isaac said, playing with one of the pups June had released from the crate, "this one could have all the makings of an outstanding service dog."

"Really?" June asked, her voice faltering so subtly that he knew he was the only one who'd caught it. He knew her so well now, and it had become more and more difficult to imagine returning to Colorado to resume his former life without her.

He hadn't realized until that moment how much he loved having her by his side.

How much he loved…her.

And yet, as he wanted to be closer and closer to

her, the thing he'd been encouraging her to do—find homes for their little furry charges—was the very thing pushing her away.

"Yes, really," Isaac continued. "He's got a calm temperament, he's alert and curious but not impulsive and he responds well to treats." Isaac beamed at June, his face full of excitement.

Ethan knew his friend was passionate about training service dogs, especially for victims of combat PTSD, and his father often donated veterinary care to keep costs down for people who needed service animals. Ethan had done the same for the time he'd been running his dad's clinic. He admired Isaac's work, but right now, all he wanted to do was to get June out of there before her kind heart let someone take a puppy, even though she didn't want to give them away.

It was so clear now. All she'd been trying to tell him was that she wanted to keep them herself. It didn't matter that she wasn't in a position to do so at the time; that could be dealt with and he would help her any way he could. All that mattered then was letting her know that he understood what was going on behind her facade of pretending to be okay.

"Isaac and Avery, would you guys mind watching the pups for a minute?"

They shared a glance and then nodded. "Of course, no problem," the two said in unison.

June set down the puppy she'd been holding and watched him carefully.

"June, would you join me for just a minute? There's something I need to talk to you about."

Her eyes narrowed but she did as he asked, taking his hand and following him to the only spot in the arena that wasn't covered in furry bodies or free dog toys and treats. He pulled her to a stop and grabbed both of her hands.

Confusion was etched into her features. "Ethan, what's wrong? Isaac was in the middle of telling me about training the male puppy to be a service dog and I..."

"How do you feel about that, June?" he interrupted. "Tell me the truth."

Her face fell and moisture sprung into her eyes. She quickly wiped away the first tear before it had a chance to fall. "It's just about the last thing I want, Ethan."

He pulled her against his chest, his heart breaking as she cried softly.

"God, June. Why didn't you just tell me that you didn't want to give them away?"

"I don't know," she said, her voice cracking in a way that made him think she wasn't telling the whole truth. "I guess it's just that you were pushing me so hard to do it, and you're the expert when it comes to dogs." She sniffed and pried her chest away from his. "I guess I felt that if you didn't think I'd be a good dog owner, then you were probably right."

"You've got it all wrong, June. If you'd have told me that what's been bothering you this whole time was that you didn't want to give the puppies up, I would have helped you find a way to keep them. I can't believe that's all it was and you kept it from me."

He thought they were having a heart-to-heart, a moment that would fix everything and get them back to normal, whatever that meant. But June was shaking her head.

He'd missed something crucial, but he had no idea what.

"No, Ethan. That's not all it is."

He was genuinely confused, and the way she was looking at him gave the impression that she was still sad and angry with him. But if that wasn't it... "Then what is it?" he asked.

More tears ran down her cheeks, making him feel like a total jerk and an idiot at the same time.

"If you can't see what's been bothering me, Ethan, then me spelling it out for you isn't going to change anything."

With those final words, she stormed off. And he knew she was very, very upset because she didn't take the puppies with her.

He wanted desperately to follow, but something in him caused him to pause. She'd made a comment in passing that morning of the snowball fight, one he hadn't paid much attention to at the time but that now stood out, marring an otherwise glowing, perfect memory.

That was it.

She'd said she needed space, time to heal from what that previous jerk did to her. And more than anything, he did not want to give her reason to lump him in with a guy like that, a guy stupid enough to let her go.

So he vowed to give her a little space, a little time, just like she asked. Maybe she would realize, as he'd begun to, that she wasn't at peace with the idea of their relationship coming to a close.

And after that passed, after her heart healed, nothing would stop him from going after her.

Nothing in the world.

Chapter Twelve

From the parking lot of her apartment building, even with tears still blurring her vision after driving aimlessly for hours, June could see her patio light blazing. The hairs on the back of her neck stood up; she did not recall flipping the switch by her back door before leaving earlier in the day.

She shut her car door and paused to grab pepper spray from her bag before making her way up the stairs to her unit. Not for the first time, but for a new reason, she wished the puppies were with her. They were still small, but their barks were deceptively loud, and lately, the little squirts had begun to put up a fuss if anyone they didn't know got too close to their mom.

Another tear slipped down June's cheek; that was how she thought of the situation. She'd basically adopted them, after all, and she still felt guilty for leaving them behind at the pet fair. Ethan would take care of them, but from the bottom of her toes all the way up to the top of her head, with every cell in her body, she hoped he wouldn't give them away that day.

But she didn't have a chance to think about regrets at the moment, because as she approached her building, June was fairly certain she caught movement on her back porch out of the corner of her eye.

She jammed her key into the lock and got in as quickly as possible, slamming the door behind her. Her back against it, she peered into her living room and down the hallway, the only light coming from a lamp on her bedside table.

"Hello?" she called, but there was no answer.

She looked out from the sliding glass door to try to see if there was someone on the patio, but the light didn't reach too far and there were shadows everywhere, so she settled for checking the lock and the dead bolt. Setting her purse on the couch, June flipped on a single lamp, checking the closets and in every potential hiding area she could think of.

But as soon as she returned to the living room and plopped down on the couch, she heard a soft knock, and it wasn't coming from the front door.

As icicles formed along her spine, she picked up the pepper spray and the golf club she kept under the couch and, one in each hand, headed over to the sliding door.

When she pressed her nose against the glass to

better see out, a face stared back at her and a blood-curdling scream erupted from her throat before she recognized who it was.

"Clayton!" she shouted, anger coursing through her veins to replace fear. Her first instinct was to call the police, but as her pulse calmed and her breathing slowed, June reminded herself that, for all his faults, he'd never been a violent man.

Clayton Miller held up his hands and turned around, showing her that he posed no threat. Convinced he didn't intend to hurt her, she dropped the golf club and unlocked the door, sliding the pepper spray into her pocket, just in case.

Hell, she thought, *I might use it just because.*

When she slid the door open, he walked slowly past her into the living room. He still stood nearly eye level with her, of course, but he'd lost weight and his thinner form didn't suit him. There were dark circles under his eyes when he looked at her, as though he hadn't slept well in weeks.

She crossed her arms over her chest, suddenly feeling a chill that had nothing to do with the January temperature. "Clayton, what in the hell were you doing on my porch?"

He cringed. "I needed to see you and my key didn't work in the lock, so I figured I'd just wait out there until you came home. Where were you, June? I've been here for hours."

She choked out a laugh, feeling sick to her stomach. "Of course your key didn't work. I had the locks changed. And after all you've done to me, your audacity continues to amaze me, Clayton. I shouldn't have to tell you this, but you don't get to ask questions like that anymore."

He looked down at his sneakers. "You're right. I... I'm sorry."

Her eyebrows rose in genuine surprise. "Well, that's the first I've heard those words since you walked out on me and took every dime I'd saved up."

"I know, June, and there's a lot I need to apologize for. I'd like to do that if you'll give me a chance."

Up until she'd found him standing on her porch, looking like something a cat had dragged up, there were a lot of things June would have wanted to say if Clayton Miller ever graced her with his presence again, and even more she'd have wanted to throw in his face. But seeing him there, she realized she no longer cared what reasons—excuses, really—he would give for leaving her and everything else he'd done.

She could finally say, with absolute certainty, that she gave less than a damn.

"I don't have anything to say to you, Clayton, and to be frank, there's nothing you can say to me that will change anything. So, if it's all the same to you, I'd like for you to get the hell out of my life for the last time."

This time, it was her choice, and she wanted him gone.

He held up a hand and she saw that his eyes were closed. "That's fine, June. I will get out of here like you asked, but there's something I wanted to give you first, if you'll let me stay just a second longer."

As he pulled an envelope from his back pocket, she tilted her chin up so she could stare down at him as though she were ten feet tall. "What's that?" she asked, not allowing her hopes to climb, not wanting to let herself wish it was what she thought it might be.

"It's...it's the money I took from you."

Her jaw dropped and she quickly pulled it closed.

"All of it," he said, holding out the paper. She stopped herself from snatching it away, opting to take it slowly instead.

"It doesn't feel like much."

"It's a check," he said. "It's not everything I took. Some of it I... I gambled away. I still owe you the rest and I plan to make good on it as soon as I can."

June rolled her eyes.

At least he'd had the courtesy to look guilty. Perhaps there was room for growth in a person as twisted as Clayton.

"Come on now, June, don't do that. It'll clear, I swear. Would I come all the way down here and give you this, knowing it wouldn't?"

"I honestly don't know, Clayton. I thought I knew you once, but then you stole everything I had and left me alone to pick up the pieces, so I really can't answer that question."

She shoved the check—if that was really what it was; she still didn't trust a word the man said—into her pocket and pointed at the door.

He gave a sad nod and turned to go.

She'd given him everything once, and he'd smashed it all, and she'd believed that if she ever saw him again, all of the rage she had felt for him would return. But standing there in the tiny living room of the only place she could afford—a place she paid for every month with hard-earned, honest money she made herself—June felt nothing but pride. Pride in herself, for putting her life back together, even if it wasn't much yet, for picking herself up off the floor and drying her tears to go to work the day after Clayton abandoned her, for telling him to hit the road when she had the chance.

She hugged herself as another chill spread through her body.

Clayton stopped, his hand on the door, and turned back. She only saw the side of his face.

"What I did was wrong, June, and you're right that it doesn't matter why. Hell, there are times when I don't even know why I did it, because some days I miss you like crazy. I know I got my own garbage to sort out, but I do want you to know that I'm sorry. I'm sorry I hurt you. If I had it to do over, I'd do things different."

With that, he opened the door. She'd thought that would be the last of him, but a second later, he was backing into her apartment as though held at gunpoint.

As he passed through the door, she saw Ethan on the other side of Clayton, shoving the man back into her living room.

"Ethan," she cried. "What are you doing?" She rushed over to where the two men stood.

Ethan's fists were curled and there was murder in his eyes. "June, who the hell is this man and why is he bothering you?"

Clayton flinched but didn't respond.

She walked over to Ethan's side and put a hand on his forearm. "It's okay. I've got this handled and you can relax."

He met her eyes. "You sure, June?" He turned to face her, jaw trembling. "I shouldn't have let you go earlier today. I should have fought for you." He tipped his chin in Clayton's direction. "I'm prepared to do that now. Just say the word."

An unexpected little flip happened in her stomach and she had to fold her lips together to keep from grinning. "I mean it, Ethan," she said, her heart going soft with tenderness toward him. "I'm fine and everything's okay. I was just telling Clayton to go on and get out."

Clayton nodded, looking relieved that he'd avoided getting punched in the face, pepper sprayed or whacked in the noggin with a golf club. Finally, the man walked out her front door, taking their dark past with him.

When June turned back around to face Ethan, even though they still had a lot to discuss, a part of her knew there would be mostly light from then on.

She walked to the door and closed it, hard, not taking her eyes off the man she loved.

"June, I have so much I want to tell you. So much I understand now that I didn't before."

"I do, too, Ethan. Oh, I shouldn't have left you earlier. Even though I was hurting, it wasn't the right thing to do, and I'm sorry."

"No, I'm the one who needs to apologize." He took both of her hands in his and led her to the couch. Recalling what had happened the last time they'd ended up there together, June's cheeks warmed and she took a deep breath. There would be time to think of that later; right then, she needed to focus on the conversation she should have had with him ages ago—the one they'd both feared, until that moment when all their walls had finally come crashing down.

For her, at least, all that remained was an exposed but ready heart, and she hoped he would offer her the same.

When they were seated, she took her time before speaking.

Ethan looked handsome, as always, but there was a little vulnerability in him just then, wearing the same hooded sweatshirt he'd put on for the pet adoption event earlier that day, his hair a little mussed, that five-o'-clock shadow she loved so much making an appearance. She longed to touch him, to reach out and run her fingers along his jaw, but there would be time for that later, she hoped.

His eyes were dark in the dim light coming from her bedroom—she still hadn't switched on any additional light, and doing so then could potentially break the spell they were under. It was one of those moments in life when she knew everything was about to change, for better or worse, and it felt as if even the quietest breath had the potential to destroy it all.

"Listen, June, I know we have a lot to say to each other, and I'd love to start if you're ready."

She offered him a tender smile, holding back from reaching out to wrap her hands in his. "No," she said, her voice firm. "Let me."

He started to open his mouth but thought better of it when he saw the determination in her expression.

"That guy that just left?" she asked, pointing a thumb in the direction of her front door.

Ethan nodded.

"That was Clayton Miller." She drew in a long breath and slowly released it. "I was in love with him for six months, so much so that I thought he would be in my life forever. We never actually talked about it, which I see now was probably a red flag, but I just assumed we would get married someday. Every moment that we weren't working, we spent together, and we both shared a dream of owning a business together."

She shook her head. "I was stupid to believe him—I see that now—but he convinced me that he'd found the perfect building for the bakery I wanted so badly, and I trusted him. I went there with him, once, to an empty store in a cute little strip mall in Dallas, and fell in love with the place."

Ethan nodded, his eyes narrowing as he followed along.

"Because I worked so much and Clay—Clayton—

had a more flexible schedule, he convinced me to transfer all of my money into his bank account so that he could make an offer one afternoon. That morning, he kissed me goodbye like always."

Ethan cringed.

"And I didn't see him again until today." Even after all that time, admitting such a thing was still embarrassing.

"Did you go to the police?" Ethan asked.

"I did, but because I'd willingly given Clayton the money and I wasn't under duress or threatened or anything at the time, there wasn't much they could do. They tried to track him down for a little while, mostly as a favor to me, I think, since this is a small town and everybody knows most of the force, but after a bit, they let it go."

She wrung her hands. "I tried to do the same, but honestly, until you came along, I was having a hard time believing that I'd ever get over that pain of being abandoned."

Ethan reached out and took her hands. "I'm so sorry he did that to you, June."

She shook her head. "And the worst part is, he made me stop trusting myself. It's a miracle I didn't extend that to everyone around me, but thankfully I didn't. I've got a lot of good people in my life that I would have pushed away if I'd have done that. But no, it was just me."

"What do you mean?" he asked, his voice gentle.

"Well, I figured that if I was that stupid once, if I trusted someone like that—someone who took everything I had without breaking a sweat—then I should never let myself get close to a man again."

"It wasn't your fault, June." The words were true, she knew, but still so hard to digest.

"So when you came along, even though I started to fall for you from pretty much the moment we met, I didn't want to let myself get too close. You seemed wonderful, but if I made such a mistake before, who was I to judge?"

"Do you still feel that way about me?"

"Of course not, Ethan," she said, willing her words to convey the extent of what was in her heart. "You have to see that."

"I do. I do see that, June, and I'm so sorry that I didn't go after you today. I'm so very sorry if I made you think I didn't care that you ran off."

"Ethan, I know you care. I can see that, even though I know you didn't really want to from the beginning."

"June, please let me explain…"

She held up a hand, then placed it back over his. "Of course, but let me finish, okay?"

He nodded, his brown eyes so warm.

"I want you to understand what happened today, when I left the pet event, I mean."

"Absolutely," he said. "I mean, I think I have some idea now, but I want to hear your story."

"Those puppies, Ethan—they mean more to me than I think you realize."

He looked like he wanted to say something but he kindly let her go on without interrupting.

"I think I've come to see them as a sort of...
symbol...for lack of a more accurate word. They've
come to represent some things for me that I hope
make sense. If it doesn't, and you think I'm crazy,
you're welcome to walk right back out that door."

"June." His voice was rigid, final. "If you'll allow
it, I will never walk out that door without you knowing
I'll be back. So, I'd love to hear what you're going to
say, but know this—I am not that man that left here a
few minutes ago. I am not him. I will never treat you
like he did. I will never do what he did to you."

Ethan swallowed, his jaw ticking in that nervous
way.

What he'd confessed certainly made it hard for her
to continue, but it also made her heart swell with joy.

"I definitely want to hear more of that," she said,
giggling, which made him laugh, too. "But what I
was saying is that, the puppies are sort of like this
representation of...well...us. Look, I know it's weird,
but they brought you into my life, and even though
we got to know each other apart from them, I always
had this sort of fear that if they went away from
me, well...you would, too. What I mean to say, or
ask, really, is...would you still be here if it wasn't
for them?"

She wanted to think she knew the answer—Lord
knew she did—but at the back of her mind there was
still an inkling of fear that, contrary to what Ethan
said, he might just walk out that door and not come
back. She hated that fear, and recognized it for what it
was—Clayton's last hold on her—the last little piece

of her trust he'd stolen. No apology could return it to its rightful place, she knew, but giving her heart to Ethan, letting him teach her to trust again, would be a pretty good place to begin.

Ethan leaned forward and took her face in his hands. "Absolutely, I would still be here, June. Absolutely. I *am* still here, and I'm not going anywhere if you don't want me to."

"Oh, Ethan, I'm so glad to hear that."

"Jessica broke my heart, too, not in the same way as yours but close enough. She abandoned me in a different way."

"Do you mind if I ask how?" June whispered.

"No, not at all. I want to tell you everything. After we'd been together for a while, I found out that she was engaged and had been cheating on her fiancé with me. I know it's not the same, but it hurt so much, and I really thought I'd never be able to trust a woman ever again. When I found out she'd been lying to me the whole time, that I'd been played like a damn fool, well, I decided then and there that I was done giving my heart away."

June nodded, her heart aching for him, but glad he'd felt close enough to her to share what had happened to him. Everything made more sense in light of that knowledge.

"So when I met you—" he smiled "—when you came crashing into my father's clinic with those two puppies under your coat, I was instantly attracted to you, and it only grew from there. I thought that if I put boundaries around our relationship, I could keep that attraction from becoming something more, but I was powerless from the beginning. I see that now, and my only regret is ever trying to keep you out."

He squeezed her hands, kissing her cheek before continuing. "I should never have compared you to Jessica in my heart, June." He shook his head. "You're nothing like her, in all the best ways possible. You are kind, sweet, openhearted and brave—so very brave—to have put your life back together after that asshole took everything from you. I can't even begin to tell you how much I admire your courage. I also should never have tried to keep from letting you in, because ever since I did, I've been happier and a better man than ever before."

His eyes bore into hers as her own moistened with tears of joy. He was saying everything she'd wanted to hear since she'd met him, and it was all she needed it to be.

"I love you, June. I love you with everything that I am."

"Oh, Ethan," she said through tears, "I love you, too. More than anything. And, just as importantly, I trust you one hundred percent, with my whole heart."

He grabbed her hands then and pulled her up from the couch and straight into his arms, swirling her around like a movie heroine. But it was better than a movie because Ethan was real. By being trustworthy, honest and willing to open his heart to her after having it broken so badly, Ethan Singh was all the hero she could ask for.

Finally, he set her back down and kissed her long

and hard, his lips conveying all the passion that had built up between them, stronger and fiercer than the first time they made love.

"One more thing, June."

"Yes?"

He looked down at her with twinkling eyes. "I'd like for you to give the puppies names. You can call them whatever you like, and they'll be ours to keep."

Her heart nearly burst. "I was so afraid you'd given them away at the adoption event... Wait, what about Neena?" June's hands flew to her mouth. "I love those puppies, and I feel like they're my babies, but I'm not going to be the kind of woman who takes a puppy from a child who's been promised one."

Ethan looked at her with enough warmth to heat her entire apartment building, plus the whole block. "That's something I was going to tell you. I got a call from Harry earlier today and he gave me some news."

June clenched her hands until her nails dug into her palms.

"It turns out Neena is severely allergic to dogs and we just had no idea." Ethan let out a deep laugh.

"Oh, my gosh," June gasped. "How awful!"

"No, no, sweetheart. It'll be fine. Harry and Amani are going to get her a rabbit instead."

Now it was June's turn to laugh. "So I really get to keep the puppies, then?"

He nodded, brushing a finger along her cheek. "You really do. And I'm sorry I was such a jerk. I was so focused on trying to figure out how to keep myself from loving you that I completely missed the fact that you'd fallen in love with those little fur balls. And I have to admit—I have, too."

She wrapped her arms around his neck and held him close for as long as she could stand. When she let go, he pressed his lips against hers, igniting a spark in her belly that she knew could only be quelled by spending the rest of her life with him.

"Well," he said, pulling his breathless mouth from hers. "You know what you have to do now."

"What?" she asked between the kisses she was busy dotting along his deliciously-scented neck. "Take you back to my bedroom and have my way with you?"

"Obviously that, yes," he growled, the low, throaty sound sending sparks to her groin. "But first, something else."

"What?"

"You have to name the puppies."

June threw her head back and laughed, all the tension and pain from the past flowing out of her. "What should I name them?" she asked.

"I can't tell you that," he said. "I was the idiot trying for so long to get you to give them away. They're ours now, but you're the one who gets to decide what we'll call them."

She bit her lip, looking up at the ceiling as she considered all of the possibilities.

"It's so hard," she said, grinning. "Naming one puppy would be difficult enough, but two?" She tossed up her hands. "That's going to take a while."

He looked down into her eyes, his own reflecting all of the joy that threatened to burst out of her. "That's absolutely fine, June. Take as long as you need."

He kissed her.

"We have all the time in the world."

Epilogue

One year later...

The weather for their wedding could not have been more different than the season in which Ethan and June had met.

There wasn't a snowflake in sight as June walked down the aisle toward Ethan, her smile shining brighter than the July sun. He didn't even try to contain the grin that spread over his mouth as he watched her draw nearer, going a little too fast—adorable—as though she could not wait to start their life together.

He could not have agreed more. Their hearts were absolutely on the same page.

She joined him underneath the archway her bridesmaids had covered in her favorite lilies, and he took her hands in his, joining them together forever as they exchanged vows.

The next hours whizzed by in a blur as they were congratulated by one family member after another. Even though the official ceremony was that day, the wedding had lasted far longer in his father's Indian tradition.

Ethan had enjoyed every moment, his heart alive and full to bursting, surrounded by family, friends, their two growing puppies, Salt and Pepper, and the most wonderful woman in the world, whose beauty in a sari was beyond all imagination.

But a part of him had to admit that he'd be relieved when it was all over and he could take his bride home.

They'd been discussing their next move for months, Ethan having accepted a new position as department head at a university in Montana. Although he hadn't pressured her, June had jumped at the chance to join him, sad to say goodbye to her hometown and the people that loved her there, but excited about the new chapter they planned to start together.

She still carried a dream of opening a bakery of her own, but she'd been willing to put that on the back burner so that she could be with him in his new state, which made the surprise he had for her that day all the more special. June wasn't expecting it at all, and he couldn't wait to tell her the news.

Finally, after they'd eaten dinner and had a moment of quiet to themselves amid the storm of attention, he managed to pull his new wife aside. The light in her eyes was incredible as she looked up at him, glowing even beyond their normal brightness.

"You look beautiful, Mrs. Singh," he said, taking her hand and leading her out to the gazebo in his parents' backyard. Fairy lights—numbering in the thousands, he was certain—had been strung up for the occasion and twinkled like June's eyes.

He pulled her close against his chest and held her there as they swayed back and forth in a slow dance. They had done the classic first dance as husband and wife, but that had been in front of everyone. This special moment, he wanted to share only with her.

"June, I will never be able to properly thank you for agreeing to be my wife."

She gazed up at him for a second and then tucked her face back into his chest. She felt so right, there against his heart, and he vowed, as he had hundreds of times before, to always keep her safe and, to the very best of his ability, as happy as she made him—though he wasn't sure such a thing was possible.

"You've made me the happiest man alive, my June, and thanks to you, I always will be." He felt her lips curve into a smile. "And you've already shown me more support than I've ever had the right to ask for."

She raised her head as they continued dancing. "What do you mean?"

"Everything," he said. "But right now I'm talking about your agreeing to come with me to Montana."

"Of course," she said. "But why wouldn't I, Ethan?" Her pretty ruby lips parted in a grin. "If that's where you're going, and that job will make you happy, then there's nowhere else in the world I would rather be."

"And I'm so thankful for that, June."

They moved slowly to the music as he enjoyed the warm night air, the stars sparkling above and the feel of a beautiful, happy woman against his body.

His woman, *forever.*

The joy he felt at that knowledge was almost too much to keep inside, so he twirled her around and around until she laughed for him, the sound of her voice as refreshing as a cool spring on a hot day.

"There's something else I want to share with you, though, Mrs. Singh."

Her nose crinkled adorably as she grinned at the sound of her new name.

"You like that, do you?"

"I do," she said, wrapping her arms around his waist. "Very much."

"Good, because I can't wait to say it to you when we're really alone."

She swatted him, then, moving her arms to his neck, pulled herself up so she could kiss him.

It was nearly impossible not to be aroused by the feel of her warm body against his. She was so beautiful in the ivory dress she'd chosen, the heart-shaped neckline showing off her gorgeous curves.

"I can't wait to get this incredible dress off you," he said. "But there's something else I wanted to tell you."

She stopped dancing and opened her eyes; they were like emerald gems when she glanced up at him. "What is it, my love?"

"June, I know we've been talking about you open-ing up a bakery someday, somewhere near my work and the home we're building."

"Yes?" Her expression was a mixture of appre-hension and excitement.

"Well, I hope you won't be upset with me, but I've sort of taken the liberty of…buying you a bakery."

She jumped back, her arms flailing to her sides. "Ethan! Are you serious?"

"Completely. And, June, it's truly amazing. Ready for operation, stainless-steel, top-of-the-line appliances, the works."

Her hands flew to her mouth. "Oh, Ethan."

She threw her body into his torso and squeezed his waist. "Thank you so, so much. I've wanted this for so long."

Unable to contain his joy at her pleasure, Ethan pulled his cell phone from the back pocket of his tuxedo pants. "Here," he said, sliding a thumb over the screen to unlock the phone. "I've got pictures for you, and specs, and everything else."

She thumbed through the photos, making approv-ing noises at each one. He'd spent ages looking for places online, calling folks in the area to see if they thought it was a good place for the kind of business his wife wanted to run. Everyone he'd spoken to had been ecstatic about the idea of a new bakery coming to their area.

And now he had confirmation that June was happy with his choice.

It wasn't possible for the day to get any better; he would have bet money on that.

"So, you like it?" he asked, needing her to put into words what he could already see on her face.

"Like it? Ethan, it's the best gift anyone's ever given me, with the one exception of this." She held up her wedding ring, tilting it so that its angles caught the light.

He'd chosen an ample round emerald circled by seed diamonds because it reminded him of her lovely eyes.

"I'm so thankful, and so happy, Ethan, but I do have one question."

"Go for it."

Her eyebrows knit. "Why did you do this, when you know I got the money back from Clayton and it's more than enough to buy a bakery?"

He'd thought long and hard about the answer to that question well before she'd asked it. He knew her money was earmarked for a bakery, and he'd taken a risk in buying the place himself, aware that she might be disappointed she hadn't done it completely on her own.

But that was just it. She wasn't on her own anymore, and he wanted her to know that without a doubt.

"I know you could have bought the bakery yourself, June, and I hope you're not angry with me for doing it as a surprise. But the thing is—I wanted you to know that I'm all in, one thousand percent. Buying that place for you, in the town we're going to call home together, was the best way I knew to show you how committed I am to this marriage."

"Oh, Ethan, how could I be angry? It's the most

wonderful thing anyone's ever done for me and I am over the moon about it."

"I thought it would be a symbol of how much I love you. Your dream was stolen before, and I wanted to give it back. I wanted you to know that you can trust me to love you well." He grabbed her hands. "Do you trust in me, June?"

"With all my heart, Ethan. With all of my heart."

With that, he swirled her around the dance floor once more.

When he set her back down, though, June looked up at him, a mischievous grin on her lips. "I have a little surprise for you, too, Ethan."

He held her out at arm's length and caught the split second her eyes flickered to her midsection.

"You're not…"

June nodded, biting her lip. "I am."

"I'm going to be a father?"

"You are," she said, bursting into tears and laughter all at once.

As he lifted her into his arms to carry her off into their future, Ethan realized he'd been wrong about one thing that night—it definitely could get better.

In fact, now that they had the promise of everything they'd wanted in a life together—it was the very best.

* * * * *

Find the next installment of Amy Woods's
PEACH LEAF, TEXAS miniseries,
coming in 2017 from Harlequin Special Edition!

Officer Wyn Bailey has found herself wanting more from her boss—and older brother's best friend—for a while now. Will sexy police chief Cade Emmett let his guard down long enough to embrace the love he secretly craves?

Read on for a sneak peek at the newest book in New York Times *bestselling author RaeAnne Thayne's* HAVEN POINT *series,* RIVERBEND ROAD, *available July 2016 from HQN Books.*

CHAPTER ONE

"THIS WAS YOUR dire emergency? Seriously?"

Officer Wynona Bailey leaned against her Haven Point Police Department squad car, not sure whether to laugh or pull out her hair. "That frantic phone call made it sound like you were at death's door!" she exclaimed to her great-aunt Jenny. "You mean to tell me I drove here with full lights and sirens, afraid I would stumble over you bleeding on the ground, only to find you in a standoff with a baby moose?"

The gangly-looking creature had planted himself in the middle of the driveway while he browsed from the shrubbery that bordered it. He paused in his chewing to watch the two of them out of long-lashed dark eyes.

He was actually really cute, with big ears and a curious face. She thought about pulling out her phone to take a picture that her sister could hang on the local wildlife bulletin board in her classroom but decided Jenny probably wouldn't appreciate it.

"It's not the calf I'm worried about," her great-aunt said. "It's his mama over there."

She followed her aunt's gaze and saw a female moose on the other side of the willow shrubs, watching them with much more caution than her baby was showing.

While the creature might look docile on the outside, Wyn knew from experience a thousand-pound cow could move at thirty-five miles an hour and wouldn't hesitate to take on anything she perceived as a threat to her offspring.

"I need to get into my garage, that's all," Jenny practically wailed. "If Baby Bullwinkle there would just move two feet onto the lawn, I could squeeze around him, but he won't budge for anything."

She had to ask the logical question. "Did you try honking your horn?"

Aunt Jenny glared at her, looking as fierce and stern as she used to when Wynona was late turning in an assignment in her aunt's high school history class.

"Of course I tried honking my horn! And hollering at the stupid thing and even driving right up to him, as close as I could get, which only made the mama come over to investigate. I had to back up again."

Wyn's blood ran cold, imagining the scene. That big cow could easily charge the sporty little convertible her diminutive great-aunt had bought herself on her seventy-fifth birthday.

What would make them move along? Wynona sighed, not quite sure what trick might disperse a couple of stubborn moose. Sure, she was trained in Krav Maga martial arts, but somehow none of those lessons seemed to apply in this situation.

The pair hadn't budged when she pulled up with her lights and sirens blaring in answer to her aunt's desperate phone call. Even if she could get them to move, scaring them out of Aunt Jenny's driveway would probably only migrate the problem to the neighbor's yard.

She was going to have to call in backup from the state wildlife division.

"Oh, no!" her aunt suddenly wailed. "He's starting on the honeysuckle! He's going to ruin it. Stop! Move it. Go on now." Jenny started to climb out of her car again, raising and lowering her arms like a football referee calling a touchdown.

"Aunt Jenny, get back inside your vehicle!" Wyn exclaimed.

"But the honeysuckle! Your dad planted that for me the summer before he...well, you know."

Wyn's heart gave a sharp little spasm. Yes. She *did* know. She pictured the sturdy, robust man who had once watched over his aunt, along with everybody else in town. He wouldn't have hesitated for a second here, would have known exactly how to handle the situation.

Wynnie, anytime you're up against something bigger than you, just stare 'em down. More often than not, that will do the trick.

Some days, she almost felt like he was riding shotgun next to her.

"Stay in your car, Jenny," she said again. "Just wait there while I call Idaho Fish and Game to handle things. They probably need to move them to higher ground."

"I don't have time to wait for some yahoo to load up his tranq gun and hitch up his horse trailer, then drive over from Shelter Springs! Besides that honeysuckle, which is priceless to me, I have seventy-eight dollars' worth of groceries in the trunk of my car that will be ruined if I can't get into the house. That includes four pints of Ben & Jerry's Cherry Garcia that's going to be melted red goo if I don't get it in the freezer fast—and that stuff is not exactly cheap, you know."

Her great-aunt looked at her with every expectation that she would fix the problem and Wyn sighed again. Small-town police work was mostly about problem solving—and when she happened to have been born and raised in that small town, too many people treated her like their own private security force.

"I get it. But I'm calling Fish and Game."

"You've got a piece. Can't you just fire it into the air or something?"

Yeah, unfortunately, her great-aunt—like everybody else in town—watched far too many cop dramas on TV and thought that was how things were done.

"Give me two minutes to call Fish and Game, then I'll see if I can get him to move aside enough that you can pull into your driveway. Wait in your car," she ordered for the fourth time as she kept an eye on Mama Moose. "Do not, I repeat, do *not* get out again. Promise?"

Aunt Jenny slumped back into her seat, clearly disappointed that she wasn't going to have front row seats to some kind of moose-cop shoot-out. "I suppose."

To Wyn's relief, local game warden Moose Porter—who, as far as she knew, was no relation to the current troublemakers—picked up on the first ring. She explained the situation to him and gave him the address.

"You're in luck. We just got back from relocating a female brown bear and her cub away from that campground on Dry Creek Road. I've still got the trailer hitched up."

"Thanks. I owe you."

"How about that dinner we've been talking about?" he asked.

She had not been talking about dinner. Moose had been pretty relentless in asking her out for months and she always managed to deflect. It wasn't that she didn't like the guy. He was nice and funny and good-looking in a burly, outdoorsy, flannel-shirt-and-gun-rack sort of way, but she didn't feel so much as an ember around him. Not like, well, someone else she preferred not to think about.

Maybe she would stop thinking about that *someone else* if she ever bothered to go on a date. "Sure," she said on impulse. "I'm pretty busy until after Lake Haven Days, but let's plan something in a couple of weeks. Meantime, how soon can you be here?"

"Great! I'll definitely call you. And I've got an ETA of about seven minutes now."

The obvious delight left her squirming and wishing she had deflected his invitation again.

Fish or cut line, her father would have said.

"Make it five, if you can. My great-aunt's favorite honeysuckle bush is in peril here."

"On it."

She ended the phone call just as Jenny groaned, "Oh. Not the butterfly bush, too! Shoo. Go on, move!"

While she was on the phone, the cow had moved around the shrubs nearer her calf and was nibbling on the large showy blossoms on the other side of the driveway.

Wyn thought about waiting for the game warden to handle the situation, but Jenny was counting on her. She couldn't let a couple of moose get the better of her. Wondering idly if a Kevlar vest would protect her in the event she was charged, she climbed out of her patrol vehicle and edged around to the front bumper. "Come on. Move along. That's it."

She opted to move toward the calf, figuring the cow would follow her baby. Mindful to keep the vehicle between her and the bigger animal, she waved her arms like she was directing traffic in a big-city intersection. "Go. Get out of here."

Something in her firm tone or maybe her rapid-fire movements finally must have convinced the calf she wasn't messing around this time. He paused for just a second, then lurched through a break in the shrubs to the other side, leaving just enough room for Great-Aunt Jenny to squeeze past and head for her garage to unload her groceries.

"Thank you, Wynnie. You're the best," her aunt called. "Come by one of these Sundays for dinner. I'll make my fried chicken and biscuits and my Better-Than-Sex cake."

Her mouth watered and her stomach rumbled, reminding her quite forcefully that she hadn't eaten anything since her shift started that morning.

Her great-aunt's Sunday dinners were pure decadence. Wyn could almost feel her arteries clog in anticipation.

"I'll check my schedule."

"Thanks again."

Jenny drove her flashy little convertible into the garage and quickly closed the door behind her.

Of all things, the sudden action of the door seemed to startle the big cow moose where all other efforts—including a honking horn and Wyn's yelling and arm-peddling—had failed. The moose shied away from the activity, heading in Wyn's direction.

Crap.

Heart pounding, she managed to jump into her vehicle and yank the door closed behind her seconds before the moose charged past her toward the calf.

The two big animals picked their way across the lawn and settled in to nibble Jenny's pretty red-twig dogwoods.

Crisis managed—or at least her part in it—she turned around and drove back to the street just as a pickup pulling a trailer with the Idaho Fish and Game logo came into view over the hill.

She pushed the button to roll down her window and Moose did the same. Beside him sat a game warden she didn't know. Moose beamed at her and she squirmed, wishing she had shut him down again instead of giving him unrealistic expectations.

"It's a cow and her calf," she said, forcing her tone into a brisk, businesslike one and addressing both men in the vehicle. "They're now on the south side of the house."

"Thanks for running recon for us," Moose said.

"Yeah. Pretty sure we managed to save the Ben & Jerry's, so I guess my work here is done."

The warden grinned at her and she waved and pulled onto the road, leaving her window down for the sweet-smelling June breezes to float in.

She couldn't really blame a couple of moose for wandering into town for a bit of lunch. This was a beautiful time around Lake Haven, when the wildflowers were starting to bloom and the grasses were long and lush.

She loved Haven Point with all her heart, but she found it pretty sad that the near-moose encounter was the most exciting thing that had happened to her on the job in days.

Her cell phone rang just as she turned from Clover Hill Road to Lakeside Drive. She knew by the ringtone just who was on the other end and her breathing hitched a little, like always. Those stone-cold embers she had been wondering about when it came to Moose Porter suddenly flared to thick, crackling life.

Yeah. She knew at least one reason why she didn't go out much.

She pushed the phone button on her vehicle's hands-free unit. "Hey, Chief."

"Hear you had a little excitement this afternoon and almost tangled with a couple of moose."

She heard the amusement in the voice of her boss—and friend—and tried not to picture Cade Emmett stretched out behind his desk, big and rangy and gorgeous, with that surprisingly sweet smile that broke hearts all over Lake Haven County.

"News travels."

"Your great-aunt Jenny just called to inform me you risked your life to save her Cherry Garcia and to tell me all about how you deserve a special commendation."

"If she really thought that, why didn't she at least give me a pint for my trouble?" she grumbled.

The police chief laughed, that rich, full laugh that made her fingers and toes tingle like she'd just run full tilt down Clover Hill Road with her arms outspread.

Curse the man.

"You'll have to take that up with her next time you see her. Meantime, we just got a call about possible trespassers at that old wreck of a barn on Darwin Twitchell's horse property on Conifer Drive, just before the turnoff for Riverbend. Would you mind checking it out before you head back for the shift change?"

"Who called it in?"

"Darwin. Apparently somebody tripped an alarm he set up after he got hit by our friendly local graffiti artist a few weeks back."

Leave it to the ornery old buzzard to set a trap for unsuspecting trespassers. Knowing Darwin and his contrariness, he probably installed infrared sweepers and body heat sensors, even though the ramshackle barn held absolutely nothing of value.

"The way my luck is going today, it's probably a relative to the two moose I just made friends with."

"It could be a skunk, for all I know. But Darwin made me swear I'd send an officer to check it out. Since the graffiti case is yours, I figured you'd want first dibs, just in case you have the chance to catch them red-handed. Literally."

"Gosh, thanks."

He chuckled again and the warmth of it seemed to ease through the car even through the hollow, tinny Bluetooth speakers.

"Keep me posted."

"Ten-four."

She turned her vehicle around and headed in the general direction of her own little stone house on Riverbend Road that used to belong to her grandparents.

The Redemption mountain range towered across the lake, huge and imposing. The snow that would linger in the moraines and ridges above the timberline for at least another month gleamed in the afternoon sunlight and the lake was that pure, vivid turquoise usually seen only in shallow Caribbean waters.

Her job as one of six full-time officers in the Haven Point Police Department might not always be overflowing with excitement, but she couldn't deny that her workplace surroundings were pretty gorgeous.

She spotted the first tendrils of black smoke above the treetops as she turned onto the rutted lane that wound its way through pale aspen trunks and thick pines and spruce.

Probably just a nearby farmer burning some weeds along a ditch line, she told herself, or trying to get rid of the bushy-topped invasive phragmites reeds that could encroach into any marshy areas and choke out all the native species. But something about the black curl of smoke hinted at a situation beyond a controlled burn.

Her stomach fluttered with nerves. She hated fire calls even more than the dreaded DD—domestic disturbance. At least in a domestic situation, there was some chance she could defuse the conflict. Fire was avaricious and relentless, smoke and flame and terror. She had learned that lesson on one of her first calls as a green-as-grass rookie police officer in Boise, when she was the first one on scene to a deadly house fire on a cold January morning that had killed three children in their sleep.

Wyn rounded the last bend in the road and saw, just as feared, the smoke wasn't coming from a ditch line or a controlled burn of a patch of invading plants. Instead, it twisted sinuously into the sky from the ramshackle barn on Darwin Twitchell's property.

She scanned the area for kids and couldn't see any. What she did see made her blood run cold— two small boys' bikes resting on their sides outside the barn.

Where there were bikes, there were usually boys to ride them.

She parked her vehicle and shoved open her door. "Hello? Anybody here?" she called.

She strained her ears but could hear nothing above the crackle of flames. Heat and flames poured off the building.

She pressed the button on the radio at her shoulder to call dispatch. "I've got a structure fire, an old barn on Darwin Twitchell's property on Conifer Drive, just before Riverbend Road. The upper part seems to be fully engulfed and there's a possibility of civilians inside, juveniles. I've got bikes here but no kids in sight. I'm still looking."

While she raced around the building, she heard the call go out to the volunteer fire department and Chief Gallegos respond that his crews were six minutes out.

"Anybody here?" she called again.

Just faintly, she thought she heard a high cry in response, but her radio crackled with static at that instant and she couldn't be sure. A second later, she heard Cade's voice.

"Bailey, this is Chief Emmett. What's the status of the kids? Over."

She hurried back to her vehicle and popped the trunk. "I can't see them," she answered tersely, digging for a couple of water bottles and an extra T-shirt she kept back there. "I'm going in."

"Negative!" Cade's urgency fairly crackled through the radio. "The first fire crew's ETA is now four minutes. Stand down."

She turned back to the fire and was almost positive the flames seemed to be crackling louder, the smoke billowing higher into the sky. She couldn't stand the thought of children being caught inside that hellish scene. She couldn't. She pushed away the memory of those tiny charred bodies.

Maybe whoever had tripped Darwin's alarms— maybe the same kids who likely set the fire—had run off into the surrounding trees. She hoped so, she really did, but her gut told her otherwise.

In four minutes, they could be burned to a crisp, just like those sweet little kids in Boise. She had to take a look.

It's what her father would have done.

You know what John Wayne would say, John Bailey's voice seemed to echo in her head. *Courage is being scared to death but saddling up anyway.*

Yeah, Dad. I know.

Her hands were sweaty with fear, but she pushed past it and focused on the situation at hand. "I'm going in," she repeated.

"Stand down, Officer Bailey. That is a direct order."

Cade ran a fairly casual—though efficient—police department and rarely pushed rank, but right now he sounded hard, dangerous.

She paused for only a second, her attention caught by sunlight glinting off one of the bikes.

"Wynona, do you copy?" Cade demanded.

She couldn't do it. She couldn't stand out here and wait for the fire department. Time was of the essence, she knew it in her bones. After five years as a police officer, she had learned to rely on her instincts and she couldn't ignore them now.

She was just going to have to disregard his order and deal with his fury later.

"I can't hear you," she lied. "Sorry. You're crackling out."

She squelched her radio to keep him out of her ears, ripped the T-shirt and doused it with her water bottle, then held it to her mouth and pushed inside.

The shift from sunlight to smoke and darkness inside the barn was disorienting. As she had seen from outside, the flames seemed to be limited for now to the upper hayloft of the barn, but the air was thick and acrid.

"Hello?" she called out. "Anybody here?"

"Yes! Help!"

"Please help!"

Two distinct, high, terrified voices came from the far end of the barn.

"Okay. Okay," she called back, her heart pounding fiercely. "Keep talking so I can follow your voice."

There was a momentary pause. "What should we say?"

"Sing a song. How about 'Jingle Bells'? Here. I'll start."

She started the words off and then stopped when she heard two young voices singing the words between sobs. She whispered a quick prayer for help and courage, then rapidly picked her way over rubble and debris as she followed the song to its source, which turned out to be two white-faced, terrified boys she knew.

Caleb and Lucas Keegan were crouched together just below a ladder up to the loft, where the flames sizzled and popped overhead.

Caleb, the older of the two, was stretched out on the ground, his leg bent at an unnatural angle.

"Hey, Caleb. Hey, Luke."

They both sobbed when they spotted her. "Officer Bailey. We didn't mean to start the fire! We didn't mean to!" Luke, the younger one, was close to hysteria, but she didn't have time to calm him.

"We can worry about that later. Right now, we need to get out of here."

"We tried, but Caleb broked his leg! He fell and he can't walk. I was trying to pull him out, but I'm not strong enough."

"I told him to go without me," the older boy, no more than ten, said through tears. "I screamed and screamed at him, but he wouldn't go."

"We're all getting out of here." She ripped the wet cloth in half and handed a section to each boy.

Yeah, she knew the whole adage—taught by the airline industry, anyway—about taking care of yourself before turning your attention to helping others, but this case was worth an exception.

"Caleb, I'm going to pick you up. It's going to hurt, especially if I bump that broken leg of yours, but I don't have time to give you first aid."

"It doesn't matter. I don't care. Do what you have to do. We have to get Luke out of here!"

Her eyes burned from the smoke and her throat felt tight and achy. If she had time to spare, she would have wept at the boy's quiet courage. "I'm sorry," she whispered. She scooped him up into a fireman's carry, finally appreciating the efficiency of the hold. He probably weighed close to eighty pounds, but adrenaline gave her strength.

Over the crackles and crashes overhead, she heard him swallow a scream as his ankle bumped against her.

"Luke, grab hold of my belt buckle, right there in the back. That's it. Do not let go, no matter what. You hear me?"

"Yes," the boy whispered.

"I can't carry you both. I wish I could. You ready?"

"I'm scared," Luke whimpered through the wet T-shirt wrapped around his mouth.

So am I, kiddo. She forced a confident smile she was far from feeling. "Stay close to me. We're tough. We can do this."

The pep talk was meant for herself, more than the boys. Flames had finally begun crawling down the side of the barn and it didn't take long for the fire to slither its way through the old hay and debris scattered through the place.

She did *not* want to run through those flames, but her dad's voice seemed to ring again in her ears.

You never know how strong you are until being strong is the only choice you've got.

Okay, okay. She got it, already.

She ran toward the door, keeping Caleb on her shoulder with one hand while she wrapped her other around Luke's neck.

They were just feet from the door when the younger boy stumbled and went down. She could hear the flames growling louder and knew the dry, rotten barn wood was going to combust any second.

With no time to spare, she half lifted him with her other arm and dragged them all through the door and into the sunshine while the fire licked and growled at their heels.

* * * * *

Don't miss RIVERBEND ROAD by New York Times bestselling author RaeAnne Thayne, available July 2016 wherever HQN books and ebooks are sold.

www.Harlequin.com

*Can secret agent Ryker Tremaine help his best friend's
pregnant widow, Marisa Hayes, overcome her grief
and make a new life—and love—with him?*

*Read on for a sneak preview of
AN UNLIKELY DADDY,
the next book in* New York Times *bestselling author
Rachel Lee's long-running miniseries
CONARD COUNTY: THE NEXT GENERATION.*

"Am I awful?"

"Awful? What in the world would make you think that?"

"Because…because…" She put her face in her hands.

At once Ryker squatted beside her, worried, touching her
arm. "Marisa? What's wrong?"

"Nothing. It's just… I shouldn't be having these feelings."

"What feelings?" Suicidal thoughts? Urges to kill
someone? Fear? The whole palette of emotions lay there
waiting for her to choose one.

She kept her face covered. "I have dreams about you."

His entire body leaped. He had dreams about her, too, and
not only when he was sleeping. "And?"

"I want you. Is that wrong? I mean…it hasn't been that
long…"

Her words deprived him of breath. He could have lifted
her right then and carried her to her bed. He'd have done
so joyfully. But caution and maybe even some wisdom held
him back.

"I want you, too," he said huskily.

She dropped her hands, her wondering eyes meeting his almost shyly. "Really? Looking like this?"

"You're beautiful looking just like that. But…"

"But?" She seized on the word, some of the wonder leaving her face.

"I don't want you to regret it. So how about we spend more time talking to each other? Give yourself some time to be sure. Hell, it probably wouldn't be safe anyway."

"My doc says it would."

She'd asked her doctor? A thousand explosions went off in his head, leaving him almost blind. He cleared his throat. "Uh…I could take you right now. I want to. So, please, don't be embarrassed. I don't think you're awful. But…please… get to know me a bit better. I want to know you better. I want you to be sure."

"I feel guilty," she admitted. "It's been driving me nuts. Am I betraying Johnny?"

"I don't believe he'd think so. But that's a question only you can answer, and you need to do that for yourself. Then there's me."

"You?" She studied him.

"I don't exactly feel right about this. After what you've already been through, I shouldn't have to explain that. I'm just like John, Marisa. Why in the world would you want to risk that again?"

She nodded slowly, looking down at where her fingertips pressed into the wooden table. "I don't know," she finally said quietly.

Don't miss
AN UNLIKELY DADDY
by New York Times *bestselling author Rachel Lee,*
available August 2016 wherever
Harlequin® *Special Edition books and ebooks are sold.*

www.Harlequin.com

THE WORLD IS BETTER WITH

Romance

Harlequin has everything from contemporary, passionate and heartwarming to suspenseful and inspirational stories.

Whatever your mood, we have a romance just for you!

Connect with us to find your next great read, special offers and more.

 /HarlequinBooks

@HarlequinBooks

www.HarlequinBlog.com

www.Harlequin.com/Newsletters

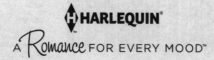

HARLEQUIN®

A *Romance* FOR EVERY MOOD™

www.Harlequin.com